A DANGEROUS DANCE . . .

Garner gripped Belasco's arm just before they hit the ground, hit it so hard it jarred Garner's teeth.

There was no time to think about it, even to cry out in pain. There was only time to try to get the damn razor out of Belasco's hand.

Garner had hold of his wrist, hard, but Belasco wasn't dropping the blade. Garner mustered all his strength and suddenly twisted onto his back, hoping to pin the sonof-abitch beneath him. But Belasco somehow wiggled out from under him and managed to get the hand with the razor free.

Garner leapt to his feet, but no faster than Belasco. Garner took a hop back and reached for his gun.

It wasn't there.

Belasco held it in his other hand, twirling it on his index finger . . .

Titles by Wolf MacKenna

DUST RIDERS
GUNNING FOR REGRET
THE BURNING TRAIL

THE BURNING TRAIL

WOLF MACKENNA

BERKLEY BOOKS, NEW YORK

THE BURNING TRAIL

A Berkley Book / published by arrangement with
the author

PRINTING HISTORY
Berkley edition / September 2002

Copyright © 2002 by Ellen Recknor.
Cover art by Bruce Emmett.

Visit our website at
www.penguinputnam.com

ISBN: 0-425-18694-6

BERKLEY®
Berkley Books are published by The Berkley Publishing Group,
a division of Penguin Putnam Inc.,
375 Hudson Street, New York, New York 10014.
BERKLEY and the "B" design
are trademarks belonging to Penguin Putnam Inc.

PRINTED IN THE UNITED STATES OF AMERICA

10 9 8 7 6 5 4 3 2 1

Prologue

With a *chink* and a *clank,* Donny Belasco hopped down from the wagon along with the other prisoners, then lined up to have his chains removed so that he could once again put in a long day's labor for the great United States of America.

Criminal, he thought, to have men out here toiling in the sun. Just criminal.

And then he smiled. He found himself very amusing.

Especially today.

Chains removed, the men shuffled in single file to several barrels of rusty shovels. Donny pulled one out and followed his mates—all dressed in wide, ragged prison stripes, all of their left ankles iron-cuffed—down to the pits.

They were making adobe bricks, just as they did several days each week. Fill a wheelbarrow with clay, push it up to the top, over and over and over. That is, if you were lucky enough to get a barrow. Most had to make do with baskets.

The men up top turned the hard clay into mud and mixed it with the proper measure of sand and quicklime and a little straw. Then another crew wheeled it to the drying yard, packed it into wooden molds, and left the molds to dry in the sun. At any given time there were acres of the curing bricks.

Exactly what they did with these bricks born of his labor—what they built, if anything, and where they took them—Donny didn't know.

He didn't care.

Especially today.

Mayfield had saved a wheelbarrow for him, and he filled it under the watchful eyes—and ready guns—of Officers Philby and Smith. Grunting, he pushed it up the ramped incline to the top. Men were everywhere, hauling water, hauling sand or quicklime, hauling clay, sweating under bright spring sun of Arizona Territory.

"Good morning to you, Mr. Caulfield," he said, rather brightly, to the officer stationed at the dumping site, and touched his forehead in a sort of salute.

"Shut up, Belasco," Caulfield replied.

"Why, certainly," Donny said, smiling. "Anything you like."

"You dumb shit," Caulfield snarled, and raised the butt of his rifle.

Donny suddenly ducked and rolled the empty barrow into Caulfield's legs, knocking them out from under him. At this preordained signal, four other men—Mayfield, Wilcox, Billings, and Cooper—launched into action, attacking the guards.

As Donny snatched away Caulfield's rifle and used it to smash the man's face with a satisfying crunch and spurt, he caught a glimpse of Pignose Wilcox doing much the same thing to Officer Philby. "Tricky Jack" Cooper had already flattened his man and was running for the hills. Mayfield and Billings weren't far behind. And the rest of the prisoners, seeing their chance, were scattering every which way.

Ah, blissful confusion, Donny thought with a brief smile.

Donny fired one shot into the back of the guard standing between himself and his mates, and ran for all he was worth.

By the time he had raced one hundred yards into the open, the guards had sufficiently recovered and started firing.

Slugs cut brush on either side of him, exploding sage and cactus alike. His lungs ached. His heart felt as if it were beating down the cage of his ribs, but still he ran.

He caught up with Pignose, saw him stumble, fall, and twitch, saw the spreading red stain, but Donny didn't alter his stride. To the left, Billings went down. To the right, Cooper yelped and fell, convulsing.

Donny just kept moving, feet pumping, heart racing, blood churning, his head about to float away it felt so light, so overjoyed.

So free.

And he laughed, laughed out loud, even while a bullet took down Mayfield, the last of his compatriots, even while the man lurched and tumbled to the ground beside him.

Donny ran, oh, he ran, and even the iron cuff felt light, as if it weren't there at all.

And when he reached the crest of the rise alone, with only the stumbling, irate guards bringing up the distant rear, their bullets by now falling far short of their mark, he saw Pignose's friend, Vince Martindale, waiting down below with five horses and a confused but expectant look, he thought that it was exceedingly good to be alive.

Especially today.

1

Hobie Hobson tossed another flake of hay into Red's manger at the moment King Garner's silhouette appeared in the doorway of the barn.

"We gonna have some grub anytime soon?" Garner asked. As always, right to the point. Right grumbly, too, if you asked Hobie.

Hobie started peeling off his worn work gloves. "'Bout fifteen minutes, Boss," he said. "Mayhap twenty. Ham okay?"

Garner turned, grunting in the affirmative, and Hobie watched him walk on up to the house. Garner stopped halfway there, his back toward Hobie, and took a another slug from his hip flask. Must be about the last one left, by the angle of the bottle.

Hobie shook his head. It was a doggone shame, if you asked him, a famous man like King Garner taken to drink. Worse than that, going fast to ruin out here on this ranch. Besides trips to the outhouse or down to the barn to yell at him or Fred or Jim, Garner hardly got off the porch anymore, let alone into town.

Hobie figured it wouldn't be much longer before Garner sank roots into the soil so deep that he got to be a tree. A regular ponderosa pine nursed on Who Hit John. Tall, but kind of weedy and apt to blow clean over at the first breath of wind.

After Hobie's daddy had died and his mama had gone back East to be with his married sister, Hobie had signed right on at King Garner's spread, which was just getting built at the time. He'd been real excited about working for a man like Garner. Here was a celebrated citizen, a man with an honest-to-goodness reputation— a man they wrote books about, by gum!— and he was slapping together a horse operation practically in Hobie's backyard!

Hobie had wanted to hear everything King Garner had to say. He'd wanted to know everything King Garner had to teach him, all about sheriffing and bravery and tracking down killers and such.

Except that King Garner didn't teach him much of anything, unless you wanted to count building barns and building houses and building corrals and taking care of livestock, and Hobie already knew how to do those. And now, with everything put up, everything tended to, it was more like he'd been hired to nursemaid a dad-gum drunk than anything else.

It was an awful big disappointment.

Muttering to himself, Hobie hiked up the hill to the house. Without comment, he crossed over the porch, passing Garner— who stared out over the broad valley, oblivious as usual— then went inside to the kitchen and put another log in the stove. Early May, but it still got nippy up here, and they kept the stove going all day and all night.

He uncovered the ham and sliced off a couple thick hunks, then thought better of it and sliced off a third. King usually liked two. Amazing how a man who drank that much could still eat like a horse. Most drunks he'd known sort of lost their appetite, but not Garner. And you'd think he'd at least put on some weight, get sloppy, but no. Hobie couldn't figure where Garner was putting it.

He set the ham in a frying pan while he hunted up the jar of applesauce he'd opened yesterday. The other hands had teased him something fearful for all the canning he'd done last season. They'd called him Miss Hobie and other names less polite—which especially hurt when you were a blonde-headed fellow and none too big or tall to begin with—but he'd had the last laugh. Nobody ate something they'd laugh at, no, sir, not while he was doing the cooking.

And nobody was laughing this year. No, next winter Jim and Fred wanted to eat something besides what they shot and cooked themselves.

He shook dried sweet corn into a pot, added water, and put that on the stove next to the ham, then dug out the pot of little green jalapeño peppers. He chopped up a couple and tossed them in with the corn, and set out three peppers each on blue enameled plates he pulled from the cupboard. Just two plates. Just for Garner and himself. The rest of the boys—that being Jim and Fred—had gone into town.

Probably to get themselves a decent meal.

"What you want me to do with all these newspapers?" he called, kicking at the stack as he passed it. He asked about every day, for all the good it did.

"Don't care," came the answer.

Well, hell. Five months' worth, give or take, of the *Zuni Gazette,* and they hadn't been so much as unfolded. They were Garner's newspapers, and nobody touched them until Garner had read them, and well, Garner wasn't reading them. He didn't pay attention to a damn thing anymore except his horses and his whiskey.

"Can I burn 'em in the stove, then?" he called, figuring that at least they'd have the kindling out of them.

"Don't care," Garner repeated.

Hobie snorted. You'd think the man who'd tracked Cherry Lazlo– the man who'd sent that murdering Jackson Woodrow to his Maker, the man who'd rounded up the Suggs gang and the Farley brothers and countless others, and who was a certified legend, some said– would give a damn about something.

Anything!

But no, Garner just wanted to sit on the porch and sip his whiskey.

"A goddamn shame," Hobie muttered, and stirred a pinch of sugar into the corn.

Zuni was coming of age, Marcus Trevor thought as he sauntered down Main Street. They'd put up a new feed store since he'd last been here, as well as a sweet shop and a tobacconist. Pretty soon, the railroad would be in here and the whole place would be growing like Topsy. Course, that would bring in all the wrong element, but he figured that was all right too.

After all, he was a U.S. deputy marshal. Without the wrong element, he'd be out of a job.

He'd just finished paying his respects at the sheriff's office, as he always did. In Zuni, that meant sitting back, putting up his boots, and having a leisurely cup of coffee or two with Tom Grayson. Good man, Grayson. Reminded him a tad of U.S. Marshal Holling Eberhart, his esteemed boss, and the man who, in his Prescott parlor, had reluctantly given Trevor this particular assignment.

Grayson had said that Trevor was a fool to try what he was about to try. Well, Eberhart had implied that, too, come to think of it.

"We'll see, Tom," Trevor had said. "We'll see." And poured himself another mug of Arbuckle's. He hadn't had such a fine cup of coffee since three days ago, at Eberhart's house.

"He won't do it, I tell you," Tom had insisted, his long mustaches bobbing with sincerity. "Not even if you chop off that long, moppy mane of yours and braid it up into a pair'a fancy reins for him. 'Sides, he's half-soused three quarters of the time, and dead drunk the other."

Trevor had just smiled.

Grayson had shaken his head and changed the subject.

Trevor reached the livery, paid his fee, and saddled up Stealth, his gray gelding. The horse was rangy– one of his parents had been a Thoroughbred, that was for certain– but then, Trevor himself was a tall fellow who needed a tall horse. Annie had named the gelding when he was a two-year-old and Marcus Trevor brought him home after one of his "business trips."

"How on earth are you ever going be stealthy on a beast like that, Marcus Trevor?" she'd asked, wiping her slim, delicate hands on a dish towel.

"Annie, my love," he'd said, settling his arm around her narrow shoulders and assuming his *listen up, be-*

cause I'm going to tell you something important stance, "Stealth is all in the mind, not the color of a horse."

She'd smacked him with the dish towel.

Well, she had a temper. But there weren't many women who'd put up with a lawman husband, especially one who was gone more than half the time. Especially one with nearly waist-length sandy hair, a thick mustache the size of a cattle car, bowed legs, and a narrow butt.

Course, she said she liked that hair of his. Said it made him look like a pirate.

He was inclined to agree with her.

One thing was for certain. Reporters didn't forget him, once they'd met him. Nobody did. He had carved himself into what the magazines called an "unforgettable character," and he was about to make the biggest news of his career.

He hoped.

It all depended on one drunken old ex-lawman.

He led Stealth from the livery barn, stuck his foot in the stirrup, and swung up, saddle leather creaking. He caught a glimpse of himself reflected in a nearby shop window, and took a moment to preen. "Goddamn," he muttered to himself. "I am one handsome sonofabitch, ain't I?"

"Hey, Deputy!" cried a grinning kid from across the street, disturbing his reverie. "You catch any crooks today?"

"Not yet," he called back with a grin. "But it's still early." He reined Stealth around and headed out of town at a soft jog.

King Garner leaned back in his porch rocker, drank the last drops from his flask, and idly debated finding the bottle and refilling it. Upon extensive thought, though, that sounded like way too much work, especially since lunch was just about on the table. Or was supposed to be. He decided against expending the energy.

Garner liked the view from his porch. He'd faced the front of the place southwest, so he'd have a clear view of the horses grazing down in the valley. The grass was green and already knee-high, and dotted with mares with their gamboling spring colts– Red's spring colts– sleek and shiny at their sides. Come nightfall, he could sit out here creaking back and forth in his rocker and watch the dying sun in a sky all full of purple and orange and pink.

He'd come up here with Red and his half of the money he and young Quincannon had taken off those hapless *bandidos* down in Indian Haunt, plus half the reward money that Lloyds of London had paid Quincannon. He hadn't wanted to take it– well, not right off– but the kid had pressed it on him.

He raised a glass to Quincannon about once a week, although he wouldn't have admitted it to him. He'd heard that Quincannon had taken his pretty little wife and moved down to Apache Springs, where he was practicing law. That was, what? Better than two years past? Quincannon or his wife wrote Garner a nice, newsy letter every Christmas and Easter– with an invitation to come and visit them anytime, door's always open– but Garner never quite got around to answering.

Funny how you sort of lost track of folks– or at least, lost enthusiasm for them– when they weren't right in front of your face.

"What the hell, Quincannon," he muttered, and touched the empty flask in his pocket. "I'd drink to you if I had anything wet to hoist."

Well, the kid had done right by both of them. Set himself up in practice, and set Garner up with a nice retirement.

He had himself a fine new stable, a crop of promising yearlings, and a new crop of nice foals.

He had Red, who was grinding his noontime hay down in the barn.

He had three men hired year-round to help him out, and he planned to hire on a couple more once they got to the point where they were breaking and training.

He'd bought this place outright, built it out of his pocket, and he still had enough money in the bank to tide him over for the next three years if he was careful with it—plenty of time for the horses to start paying for themselves.

Just like he'd always pictured it. Just what he'd yearned for.

So why the hell was he so bored?

And why was he drinking the way he was?

He had everything he'd wanted: the best stud horse in the whole damn Territory, some of the finest mares, a place of his own where nobody bothered him and nobody came whining to him with their problems, expecting him to solve them.

He'd solved enough of other people's problems, solved enough of his own, seen enough blood and torment and grief to last a man ten lifetimes.

And he was going to be fifty.

Oh, it was a few years off yet, but he saw it looming on the horizon just as sure as a circling wolf waiting to pounce. Fifty goddamn years old. Forty had been bad enough, but fifty? What the hell would he do then? What the hell would he be *able* to do?

Age was already creeping up on him. When he was a younger man, he'd laughed at those older hands who took so long to get up in the morning, stomping their feet or working the cricks out of their backs or necks or binding up their ruptures. Now he knew what it was to have your whole body wake up in a small series of crackling or painful or, at the least, uncomfortable events.

And he had no doubt that it was going to get a whole lot worse.

"Hobie!" he shouted, suddenly angry. "Lunch ready yet?"

"Keep your darn shirt on," came the mumbled reply.

"I heard that," he shouted back.

"Didn't hear *me*, though," said a new voice.

Garner twisted toward it, relaxing only marginally when he saw the familiar face. U.S. Deputy Marshal Marcus Trevor rode the rest of the way up to the porch and just sat there on his horse, smirking.

"What you want?" Garner asked curtly. That horse of Trevor's must have been half-cat, it was so quiet!

"And a pleasant howdy-do to you, too, King," Trevor said. He was a tall man, about as tall as Garner, but only thirty or so, way too young to be a U.S. deputy marshal. That was how Garner had met him, through Holling Eberhart. Holling was an old friend, currently on the payroll of the federal government, but Garner didn't hold that against him. Much.

Unlike either Garner or Holling, Marcus Trevor was in the prime of his life whether he knew it or not. But wasn't there a little more gray shot through that long, curly, sand-colored mop of his since the last time Garner had seen him? His eyes looked a tad more raggedy too, like spiders had been spinning at their corners.

Showboating would do that to a fellow. Trevor had a reputation, but not an honestly deserved one, if Garner was any judge.

Trevor swung down off the gray, his hair bouncing against his back and shoulders with a life of its own, and neatly tossed his reins around a porch post. "Gonna ask me up?"

Garner shrugged.

"Cranky bastard, aren't you?" Trevor muttered as he mounted the steps.

Hobie stuck his head out the door, then grinned wide. "Hey, Deputy Trevor!" he said eagerly. "It's me, Hobie Hobson! I met you last fall, remember? When you was up here with Marshal Eberhart. You stayin' for chuck? Fried ham with applesauce. And sweet corn. We got plenty."

Trevor looked at Garner, who looked away, grumbling, "Aren't you just a tad free with my grub, feedin' every stray sonofabitch that wanders in?"

"Might's well," Trevor said loudly, pretending not to hear. "Thank you kindly, Hobie."

Trevor pulled out a straight chair, flipped it around, and sat down on it, arms flopped over the backrest. He took off his hat, rubbed the back of his neck thoughtfully, then said, "Got to hand it to you, King. I fully expected to come out here and find you vamoosed."

Garner tipped his head. "Why?"

Trevor ignored the question. He gazed out over the valley. "No, I think you got the right idea. Just hide out up here, play with your horses, and drink like a fish. Keep you out of trouble."

Garner had known he was pretty well sauced, but he hadn't figured it showed. Plus which, he must be more dithered than he'd thought, because he couldn't make heads nor tails out of what Trevor was saying.

He grunted indignantly, pushed back his hat, and said, "What the Sam Hill you talkin' about?"

Trevor blinked twice, then his eyes narrowed. "You don't know, do you?"

"Dammit, Marcus! Know what?"

"Don't you get the newspapers?"

Garner rolled his eyes at the same time that Hobie's droll, "Yeah, but we just burn 'em up in the stove," carried out the door.

Trevor and Garner started at each other for a second, and then Trevor broke the silence. "Donny Belasco busted out of Yuma."

Something inside fell and shattered. There was a muttered curse, and then the screen door banged open.

"D-did you say Donny Belasco?" Hobie asked, eyes big as saucers, a dishrag hanging limply from his hands. "*The* Donny Belasco? Boss, didn't you put him away about ten years back?"

The men on the porch all but ignored him.

Garner said, "When?"

"Two weeks this Thursday," replied Trevor. And then he hurriedly added, "Now, King, don't go gettin' yourself in an uproar. Nothin' you can do. Marshal Eberhart just sent me up here to check and see that you was all right, that's all. Besides, Belasco's gone south."

"Mexico?"

"No. I mean, he's stayin' to the south, so far as we can tell," Trevor added. "Somebody saw him in Tucson last week. Two somebodies. One was the soiled dove he sliced up. Other was the drunk he tripped over in the alley on his way out."

Garner stared at his hands. "Old habits die hard," he muttered. He looked up. "She live?"

"Just long enough to say who it was did it, though we would'a known it just by lookin' at her," Trevor replied. Now it was his turn to look away. "She . . . she was cut up awful bad."

Garner didn't say anything for a while. He thought about Donny Belasco, about the fresh-faced boy whose habit it was to routinely slice up any gal he could get his hands on. No, not any gal. Just doves, at least back in the old days. Just young, pretty ones.

It was always the same. He never raped them. That would have been too ordinary for somebody like Donny Belasco. No, he carried a razor and he used it to slice off their ears, then . . .

Garner shuddered.

"I hoped I could forget about that sonofabitch when I handed him over at Prescott," he said, although the little bastard was never far from his mind, even after all this time.

Trevor nodded. "I hear you talkin'."

"Should've hanged him," Garner muttered, more to himself than to Trevor.

"Yeah," Trevor answered.

Garner had meant that he should have hanged him personally, been judge, jury, and executioner. He didn't know what Trevor thought.

"How'd he do it?" Garner asked after a moment. "Escape, that is."

Trevor ran his hand over his face. "Work detail. Five of 'em made a run for it. They had horses waitin' with a sixth feller on the other side of the ridge. Donny was the only one what made it."

He turned back toward the door. "Hobie, that ham ready yet? I could eat a grizzer."

Hobie snapped back to attention. "Half a minute, Deputy. Comin' right up." The screen door banged behind him, and they both heard him mumble, "Donny Belasco. Geez Louise."

2

Late that night, when the hands were asleep and Marcus
Trevor had long since taken his leave, King Garner sat
at his kitchen table, smoking a cigarette and going
through back issues of the *Gazette*. The ones that Hobie
hadn't burnt up, anyhow.

Marcus Trevor hadn't told him the half of it, according to the papers. And if Garner knew newspapers, there
was a great deal that even they left unsaid.

It seemed like Donny Belasco was up to his old
tricks, all right, except he was branching out. The papers reported the killing of the whore down in Tucson,
but also made frequent references to another murder:
this one of a young rancher's wife down in Dog Leg.
She'd been badly cut up, just like the others Donny Belasco had left behind. And like the hooker, she'd bled to
death.

It was probably better that way.

The paper showed Donny Belasco the way he'd been

when Garner hauled him in, and then showed him the way he was now. Not much difference, aside from the prison uniform and the number.

He didn't even look much older, aside from a more chiseled appearance, a certain loss of baby fat. Still the handsome, innocent, boylike face, a face that said, "Trust me, I'm your son, your sweetheart, your brother, I'll never hurt you."

Faces lied.

There seemed to be quite a bit of speculation about the man who'd helped him escape. Nobody had seen his face, and the two of them had galloped away, leaving behind the horses meant for the prisoners who didn't make it.

Some said it was "Reckless Roy" Branch, who was an old partner of Jubal Billings, one of the slain prisoners. Some said it was more likely Cam Cooper, brother to one of the other prisoners that had died during the break. Some even said it was old Juan Alba, who had once plagued the banks and stages of southern Arizona, come back from the dead—or up from Mexico.

Garner figured that they were pretty much full of horse piss if they were pinning it on Alba. Nobody'd heard a peep out of him in the last five years. And besides, he was even older than Garner was.

Now, Garner hadn't had a drop since Marcus Trevor had brought him the news. Hobie had been eyeballing the bottle all through the afternoon and evening, but didn't say anything when its level failed to descend. Garner knew he was curious, though. Curious enough that Garner figured the kid knew what he was thinking, and just might try to tag along.

Therefore, Garner had determined to leave at night. It would be tomorrow afternoon, maybe later, before a concerned Hobie tracked down Marcus Trevor and reported that he'd gone out after Donny Belasco. At which point, he imagined, Trevor would rip off his hat, toss it on the ground, and give it a good stomping. Old Man Garner mucking up the works, he'd say, trying to do the job of a young buck, a job nobody in his right mind would have asked him to do.

But Garner figured differently.

Somebody had to go get Donny Belasco. Way back when, the legal boys had let him off easy, said he was crazy and sentenced him to life. That was trying to keep a rabid wolf on a chain and hand-feed him grapes, as far as Garner was concerned.

Now they'd not only dropped Belasco's leash, but they'd let him roam around out there for two whole weeks while they chased their tails and their paperwork. They had two dead girls to show for it. Maybe more. Donny Belasco might have been crazy as a June bug, but there were worse things than crazy.

Pure evil, for instance.

This time, Garner was going to catch him, and he was going to kill him. Cut out the poison once and for all.

Marcus Trevor wouldn't like it and neither would Marshal Eberhart, but Garner figured there wouldn't be much they could do about it. It would be his word against that of the authorities—"He resisted me, Marcus, I'll swear to it!"—and most sane folks would just be damn glad there was one less homicidal lunatic out there for them to worry about.

He stood up and hoisted his saddlebags, already packed full, and a couple of canteens, already filled, although just with well water. Funny thing, the urge for whiskey had just fled him, plain and simple, when Trevor brought him the news.

Maybe he was just too much like an old cow dog in

that he needed a job to do, Garner thought as he quietly let himself out of the house and crossed the porch. Maybe it was needing to be needed, even if Trevor claimed they didn't need him at all, had practically said he was useless.

"You'd best stay hid out up here," Trevor had told him at least three times. "Marshal Eberhart thinks so, too. Why, that Belasco's round-the-bend loco. And who knows, he might want revenge on the man what brought him to justice. You're smart to just stay put, King, right smart. Pass the peppers there, Hobie."

Well, let Trevor think what he wanted.

Garner opened the barn door, slipped inside, and lit a lantern. Red woke at the soft sound and the light, and rumbled a low nicker.

"There, boy," Garner said, smiling. "Ho, boy."

He went to the stud and rubbed his forehead. They'd really been through some times, hadn't they? Hell, he'd chased Red all over the Territory and down into Mexico a few years ago, and it had taken more than six months— and a lot more lives—before he'd finally got him back.

It occurred to him that he'd shed more blood, seen more death, in those six months than he had in all his years as sheriff in Medicine Rock.

Damned horse thieves.

He gave the stallion a final pat on his glossy neck. "Not this time, old son," he said softly. "You already cost me too dear."

He stopped in front of Faro's stall. Faro was a bright coppery bay, a good, big, sturdy gelding that Garner had ridden all during his hunt for Red. He'd turned out to be such a damned nice horse that Garner didn't have the heart to sell him off once he got his ranch money, even if he couldn't breed.

Garner opened the stall door, clipped on the lead, and led Faro out.

"Got us a little work to do, old son," he said quietly as he shook out the saddle blanket, then laid it in place. "Time I worked some of that fat off you, anyhow."

Faro snorted softly, as if to say that was fine by him.

By daybreak, Garner and Faro had journeyed a good way down out of the mountains, and had made camp on the edge of an old beaver meadow. Garner wasn't feeling any too chipper. His head hurt and his stomach felt achy, and his joints were complaining loudly. He'd planned to catch a couple of winks—maybe an hour or so—and then move on. Tucson was, after all, a fair piece off. No telling where the little bastard had gotten to from there, but it was a place to start.

Now, as much as Garner hated to admit it, he missed having company on the trail. And specifically, he missed Pike, the old coot he'd traveled with last. Pike couldn't shut up to save his life and he cheated at cards, but by God, at least he could cook halfway decent, he was absolutely fearless, and he was a breathing body.

Well, he had been up until his neck met with Jackson Woodrow's sword.

It still made Garner mad just to think about it. Awful sad, too. Poor old Pike.

Garner hobbled Faro and turned him out, laid himself down on a likely-looking patch of grass, and pulled his hat down over his eyes.

Hobie Hobson kept his eyes on the ground.

Dad-gum that King Garner, thinking he could just take off on some wild-goose chase and not let anybody tag along!

Oh, Hobie knew right off the bat where Garner was going and why. Thought it was a "maybe" by the time Deputy Trevor set into telling one of those stories of his—this one about how, single-handed, he had stopped the Tredwell gang up in the San Francisco Peaks: an oft-told story, which, after Trevor had told it the last time, Garner had later confided to Hobie was a bunch of horseshit. Hobie was too polite to let on, though. Garner was too drunk.

Hobie had known for fairly sure about Garner's plans by the time Deputy Trevor rode out, hair swinging behind him. And he'd known it for absolute certain by four in the afternoon, when the level on that whiskey bottle hadn't sunk down even a smidgen.

He just hadn't expected that Garner would ride out in the dark, hard middle of the night and leave him behind, that was all.

Well, if Garner thought he could get away, go off, and have an adventure all by himself, he had another think coming.

Hobie's daddy hadn't taught him to track for nothing. He could practically trail a bumblebee through a blizzard, and he could sure as hell trail a big man on a big horse down a mountainside.

He smiled. All those boring years of putting in fences, building corrals and the house and the barn were forgotten. Finally, he was going to see King Garner in his true element. He was going to see, close up, what a real hero did.

Oh, he'd read about it, of course. There had been exactly three dime novels written about his illustrious boss. He had all of them, and he kept them hidden under his mattress. After all, he'd seen what Garner had done to a copy of *King of the Wild Country* that a hapless—

and former—hand had brought out to the ranch, and then had had the poor sense to show to Garner.

The book had lasted exactly one and a half minutes—the time it took Garner to walk it to the outhouse and drop it down the hole.

"Funny," Hobie muttered to no one in particular, except maybe his good buckskin gelding, Fly. "If somebody was to write a whole book about me—let alone three of 'em—I'd be downright curious to see what they had to say."

Still, Hobie figured that those books stretched the truth a bit. After all, he'd never heard his boss say anything close to "Hold up, you villains, and sheath your weapons!" or "This rain of gunfire be damned! They'll not shoot me today!"

In the books, King Garner frequently said those things, or things like them.

But some of it—the stories themselves—sounded like they had a little truth to them, all right. Hobie just wanted to see for himself. Maybe even get in on a little of that hero business himself, just to see what it felt like.

After all, times were changing. His sister lived all the way across the country, in New Jersey—and his mama with her—and she wrote that they were going to have electric wiring and real electric lights sometime in the next year or so.

There were already honest-to-God telephones in the sheriff's office and the office of the *Gazette* back in Zuni, not to mention the saloon and the mercantile and a few private homes. And he'd heard—although he hadn't exactly seen it for himself—that the Michaelsons and the Oatmans and the Donovans all had flush toilets right smack in the house!

It didn't seem sanitary, somehow.

But it was the age of wonders, or close to it. Hobie had a feeling that this was just the beginning, although of what, he wasn't quite sure. But he also thought that with all these new inventions coming at a man right and left, with the railroads branching out more all the time, he was witnessing the start of a whole new era—and the passing of another.

King Garner's, to be exact, and the era of men like him.

Hobie was only twenty-two, but he was nobody's fool. He wanted to be a witness to the deeds of one great man before the world had none left.

And besides, Garner needed him. Why, the man would likely starve to death on his own!

Hobie ducked in the saddle to avoid a low-hanging pine bough, and kept on following the trail.

Garner woke with a start, and instantly realized that he'd slept far too long. The sun was high overhead and blindingly bright. Close to noon, dammit. And he still felt sick as a dog, all woozy in the head. Kind of like he'd been on a real long drunk.

Which, of course, he had.

"Why didn't you wake me up?" he snarled at Faro, who looked up from his grazing just long enough to snort, and then got back to business.

"Thought I just did," said a voice behind him, and Garner rolled to his stomach and had his Colt free of its holster before he saw who it was.

"Dammit, Hobie!" he shouted, and holstering his gun, hauled himself slowly to his feet. "You realize you just about got yourself shot?"

Hobie put both hands, palms down, on the saddle horn and said, "But I didn't, did I? Where you rushin' off to in such a toot, and in the middle of the night? As if I didn't know."

Garner ignored the pains and pricklings in various parts of his still half-asleep body. He picked up his saddle and walked through the weeds toward Faro, thinking that everybody and his Uncle Fred was doing a real good job of sneaking up on him lately.

"If you're so all-knowing," he said, "then you ought'a know I don't need your company, Hobie. Don't want it." He settled the blanket over Faro's back, then swung the saddle up and rocked it into place.

"You know you can't cook worth a tinker's damn," said Hobie.

"It's not the cookin' I'm concerned with," Garner said testily, and reached under Faro's belly for the girth strap. The movement made him a touch dizzy, and he had to wait a second, after he straightened up, for the world to stop wobbling.

Hobie patted his saddlebags. "Got me two big ham sandwiches here in my pack," he said. "With mustard and butter on 'em. Yessir, two thick ol' sandwiches, plenty of fat, just the way you like 'em. Got some jalapeños and two big slices of that blueberry pie I made for your supper last night."

Garner paused. His stomach was growling, all right. Worse since Hobie had started talking food. And the kid could cook up a storm.

Maybe even better than old Pike, God rest him.

But Garner said, "Quit trying to bribe me, Hobie. Go on back home." He gave the girth strap a final tug, then secured it.

"Why, I bet you only brought the fixin's for corn dodgers," Hobie said, a little too patiently for Garner's taste. "Plumb awful, greasy old things, corn dodgers, even when they're fresh fixed. And mayhap you brought some jerked venison. But then, there weren't too much at the ranch. Probably won't last more than a day or two. And I can hear your stomach gurglin' clear over here, Boss."

Garner dropped his arms—and with them, the bridle—from Faro's head and hooked the headstall over the saddle horn. He stood there a moment, then walked back toward Hobie.

"Fine," he said angrily. "But after we eat, you go." He turned back toward Faro. "And don't you roll with that damn saddle on!"

Faro just kept grazing.

3

Garner had good reason to be cranky, because directly after lunch he puked up all he'd eaten and then some.

That meal had sounded awful good while Hobie was talking about it, and tasted even better while Garner was wolfing it down. But after it sat in his gullet for about five minutes, it had turned into something wholly demonic.

"Why aren't you sick?" Garner had groused weakly once he figured his stomach was empty. The taste of bile mixed with blueberries was in his mouth, and it felt like somebody had washed the whole inside of his head and nose with some kind of diluted, slow-working acid.

Hobie wrung out another cloth in the cool water he'd carried up from the old beaver creek. "'Cause I'm not the one who just all of a sudden decided to stop drinkin'," he said, and laid the cloth over Garner's forehead. "Thing like that's bound to be a shock to a man's system."

Garner reached to snatch the cloth away, then thought better of it and let his hand drop into the weeds. "I still say you poisoned me," he grumbled.

Wisely, Hobie didn't answer.

Now, although Garner was still sick as a dog, he was beginning to see things a bit more clearly. He'd been half-soused for roughly the past year and a half, and it was a half-sozzled Garner who'd made the decision to ride out, big as you please, after Donny Belasco—just like he was still thirty and in the prime of life, just like he still wore a badge.

Just like he still cared.

But the truth was, he did care.

Not in the way he supposed Hobie thought that he did. He knew Hobie idolized him, and he couldn't help but think a tad less of the boy for it. After all, who the hell but some dumb kid would put the likes of him on a pedestal? It made him itchy, made his skin crawl.

But if Hobie thought Garner was going down south to right some cosmic wrong just for the sake of doing it, if he thought that Garner was some goddamned knight about to run out and slay a dragon just because it needed doing, he was dead wrong.

He was going to exterminate Donny Belasco, pure and simple.

He remembered the day he'd arrested Donny, on the outskirts of Phoenix. He remembered how he'd nearly killed the kid doing it, and the way the slimy little bastard had taunted him. But he hadn't killed him, no, sir. He'd been a sworn officer of the law, and he hadn't finished Donny, although he'd had plenty of cause.

No, Garner had gritted his teeth and dragged Donny Belasco all the way up to Prescott, bound and gagged and tied across his saddle like a sack of spuds. And all the time, Garner cursed the air he breathed because Donny Belasco was breathing it, too.

He'd known one of those pretty little gals that Donny had done in, all those years back. Not very well, but he'd known her. He still thought about her sometimes, thought about her smile and those dimples.

Junie Corcoran was her name. Pretty little brown-haired Junie.

Jesus, she was only eighteen.

No, his argument with Donny Belasco went way beyond all those altruistic notions that he figured Hobie had in his head. His argument with Belasco was wholly personal.

He sat up, the cloth on his head falling to the ground. "I'm all right," he said, even though the meadow seemed to be bobbing up and down like an ocean of grass. "Go home."

Hobie sniffed. "You sound like you've got the ague. Or worse. And I ain't leavin'."

For somebody who Garner was pretty sure idolized him, the kid was awfully damn argumentative.

"Then I'm leaving," Garner said, and clambered uneasily to his feet.

As Garner stood there, wobbling, Hobie crossed his arms and said, "Then go, Boss. Nobody's holdin' you here."

"Doing it right now," Garner snapped, and fell to his knees.

Hobie made no attempt to come to his aid. He just stood there, arms still crossed, and said, "You're not makin' much progress, Boss. You want I should roll you some closer to your horse?"

"Goddamn it," snarled Garner, and promptly threw up again.

• • •

By mid-afternoon, they had traveled some distance. Hobie was in the lead. He figured that they were at least going generally lower in altitude, because the trail seemed more down than up. He hoped he was going the right way. Oh, he knew it was south, but he hoped the old game path he was following would dump them off at something Garner recognized.

Hobie was hopelessly lost, if the truth were known. His daddy had taught him to track, all right, but most all their excursions had been to the north or the east of Zuni. Besides, tracking had nothing to do with being a trail guide, and Hobie had never been down this way before.

And Garner was no help, although Hobie hoped that if he led them too far afield, Garner would say something. Anything!

Why, Hobie was afraid to look back just to check and see if Garner was still there! He knew Faro was. He could hear the gelding's hoofbeats plodding along behind him. He chanced a quick look over his shoulder– the first one he'd dared in over an hour– and all he got for his concern was a barked "I'm all right, dammit!"

He thought about the note he'd left for Jim and Fred, and he wondered how long it would take them to figure out that they could bust the lock off the pantry door. He figured that he could just kiss his preserves and canned goods good-bye. There probably wouldn't be a single jar of strawberry jam or green peas or pickled beets or applesauce left by the time he got back.

And all those jars would probably be left in the sink to draw flies while Jim was pouring the last of the peaches down his throat and Fred was guzzling the last of the jarred tomatoes. Probably still be there, all dried up and buggy, when he and Garner got back home.

He snorted. Goddamn pigs, that's what Fred and Jim were.

Now his boss, that was another matter. Garner just ate what you set in front of him, no questions, no arguments. Hobie liked that about him. But otherwise, he was sure a strange man. Snappy as a crawdaddy one minute, almost nice the next. You just couldn't tell about Garner.

The only thing you could count on was that he was better to horses than he was to people. He always had Hobie and Jim and Fred feeding or grooming or cooling out some horse or another; always had them pulling horseshoes or putting them on, filing down hooves or floating teeth, or bringing in the mares if there was even a hint of snow in the sky. Was that black mare favoring her left front just a tad? Was the new bay foal nursing as eager as it should?

And that stud horse, Red? Why, you'd think that cayuse was Garner's own son! He'd seen Garner just stand down by Red's corral, talking to the horse and petting him or brushing him for hours. He almost always carried treats—carrots or pippins or even lump sugar—in his pocket for Red.

Well, Red was an awful nice horse. Hobie would admit to that much. And if the story in the last King Garner book was true, he guessed Garner had gone through hell and high water just to hang onto him.

He would've liked to ask Garner about it, get the story from the horse's mouth, as it were, but there was no way he'd broach the subject. Still . . . Cherry Lazlo and Jackson Woodrow! Just thinking about those names– and their accompanying reputations– made the hair on the back of Hobie's neck stand up.

Not that Donny Belasco wasn't just as bad. Hobie had been just a kid, in the seventh grade maybe, when Donny got sent away to Yuma, and the stories about the things he'd done had been so rank that Hobie's mama burned the newspapers rather than let him read them.

Kids talked, though. They talked about Donny Belasco a lot. And none of it was good.

But then, kids exaggerated. Could Donny Belasco have cut up those girls as bad as they said?

Something in Hobie wouldn't let him believe it, wouldn't let him believe that any human person could slice up another that way. Wild animals clawed each other, sure, but they didn't study on it the way that Donny Belasco was reported to. Animals did it for food. Donny Belasco, they said, did it for pleasure.

Unbidden, a shudder traveled through him.

Maybe this trip wasn't such a good idea after all.

Three days later, they rode into Phoenix.

Hobie was excited to see the town, and had set out right away once they got settled at the hotel, but Phoenix would have to go a long way to get Garner enthused. It had neither the back-East elegance– nor the wild and wondrous Whiskey Row– of Prescott. And it didn't have the Old Mexico pueblo charm of Tucson.

However, it was a reasonably sizable settlement, even if it looked just like everyplace else, with hotels and decent food and a Goldwater's. That was pretty much all Garner cared about.

He'd settled into the notion that having Hobie ride along was a halfway decent idea, even if it hadn't exactly been his. The boy was company, after all. Plus, he mostly shut up when you told him to, and he was a real fair hand with a skillet.

Garner hadn't yet figured out what to do with Hobie once he cornered Donny Belasco, though. Donny wasn't above much. Three men, all civilians, had been shot or sliced up when Garner took him in the last time– right down the road, on what at that time had been the far end of Washington Street– and one of them had been crippled for life.

It was a good thing that Donny wasn't near as good with a gun as he was with a blade, or they'd all have been mincemeat that day.

Garner took himself to Goldwater's and bought a few things for the trail: canvas water bags, extra boxes of cartridges, a pack rig, and the like, and while he was at it, a new shirt, a white one with plain stitching and little red embroidery things on the points of the collar. He hadn't had a new shirt in a long time.

He didn't stop to pick up foodstuffs, though. Hobie could care of that part. After all, he'd be doing the cooking.

Garner stopped in at a dealer's and bought a decent pack mule, a tall roan named Charlie Blue, and arranged to have him led down to the livery where they'd left Faro and Fly. Then he stopped in at Southwick's Café and had himself a leisurely cup of coffee.

He did all of these things without a soul recognizing him.

King Garner had gone all his adult life with people knowing who he was, pointing him out in the street and coming up to shake his hand.

Or running the other way.

He'd always thought he hated it, thought he always would. But right this minute, on a sidewalk full of people, all of them strangers who were bustling along and thinking about anything and everything except King Garner, he kind of missed it.

Hobie caught up with him a block from the hotel, and took the pack rig from him and shouldered it. Garner was glad to get rid of the damned thing.

"You buy us a mule or a burro to put underneath this?" Hobie asked, all breathless excitement.

"You make a shoppin' list yet?" Garner asked after he gave a grunt in the affirmative.

"Already been to the general store," Hobie said, his enthusiasm undaunted. "Stuff'll be ready to pick up the first thing in the mornin'." And then he stopped to stare across the street. "Hey, Boss? Ain't that Deputy U.S. Marshal Trevor wavin' at you?"

"Aw, shit," Garner muttered.

It was Trevor, all right, crossing the street, dodging horses and wagons, and flagging them down. The last thing Garner wanted was some overeager lawman giving him yet another lecture on how he should just stay home and whittle in his rocking chair, and how catching criminals was a young man's game.

Especially since it was true.

"Hell's bells," Trevor said when he stepped up on the walk. "Thought you were gonna walk right on past. You goin' deaf there, King?"

Garner was tempted to pound him, but his hands were full of packages.

"What's the trouble, Marcus?" he asked tersely. "Can't a man go to town for supplies anymore without some damn lawman asking him his business?"

Trevor cocked his head. "Don't believe I asked you anything yet there, King. Seems to me you sure traveled a good long way for your supplies, 'specially since you could get most anything in Zuni. And since when have you got a grudge against lawmen?"

Garner didn't say anything, but that idiot Hobie sure did. He said, "We're on the trail of Donny Belasco, Deputy Trevor. We're gonna get him, too!"

Garner ground his teeth, but Trevor broke out in a big, self-satisfied grin. "That right, King?" he asked. "I knew you couldn't stay out of the game for too long. Can't teach an old dog new tricks, I always say."

"Old dog?" Garner growled.

Trevor threw an arm around Garner's shoulders. "Now, King, it's just a figure of speech. Should have said that you can't teach a seasoned huntin' dog to stay under the porch when there's a coon in the woods."

Garner shook off Trevor's arm. "What's the problem, Marcus?" he said quietly through gritted teeth. "You all of a sudden decide you don't like your face arranged the way the Good Lord made it?"

Trevor took a step back and held up his hands, palms out. "Maybe we should just start over."

"Maybe so," said Garner tersely. "You go back up to Zuni, and I'll get on with my business."

Trevor's face hardened. "You're makin' this damned hard, King. All I wanted to do was— "

"All you wanted to do was to tell me to go back to sippin' whiskey on my porch," Garner snapped. "All you wanted to do was to tell me to leave Donny Belasco to you boys. Didn't you ride clear up to my place to tell me so?"

Garner dropped his parcels with a resounding thud and leaned toward the deputy. "Well, I'm here to tell you that I can still do my job better than four of the likes of you, *Deputy* Trevor, even if I have been sittin' on my butt for almost three years, and been out of the law game longer. Donny Belasco is my responsibility. I plan to stop the damn lunatic before he does any more damage than he already has."

"You done yet?" Trevor asked after a moment. He hadn't budged an inch.

Garner straightened. "I reckon."

Trevor dug into his pocket and pulled out a tin whistle, a compass, forty-six cents change, a token for Marie's House of Pleasure up in Prescott, and finally, a scratched and tarnished silver badge, which he held out to Garner.

"All I wanted to do was pin this on you," he said. "If you're gonna go runnin' around, wavin' your pistol willy-nilly, lookin' under rocks and claimin' it's your damn job, then you'd best be legal about it."

Garner blinked. "What?"

Hobie enthusiastically piped up. "What about me, Deputy?"

They both ignored him.

Suddenly, it all clicked into place like the lid on a watch case. Garner snarled, "You pernicious, sneaky-ass sonofabitch! All that talking you did up at my place, about how I should just lay low until you boys caught him! All those nasty words about me going deaf and old dogs and—"

"That's me," replied Trevor, straight-faced. He pinned the lackluster badge on Garner's vest. "Oh, I'm a sly one, all right. Anyhow, that's what my Annie keeps tellin' me." Trevor twisted his head, admiring the badge on Garner's chest. "Looks right natural, if I do say so. Reckon you remember what I got to say when I give out one'a those, so I ain't gonna waste the breath. Just say, 'I do.'"

"Screw you," Garner grumbled.

"Close enough," said Trevor.

"Don't I get to be deputized?" Hobie practically wailed. "I'm goin' after Belasco, too."

Trevor shrugged and shook his head. "Sorry, kid. Ain't got but the one on me. You vouch for Hobie, here, King?"

"No," Garner said.

Hobie looked like Garner had just smacked him, but Trevor smiled.

"Reckon that means yes, Hobie." Trevor reached over and skinned the badge off Garner's vest, then handed it to Hobie.

The kid stared at it as if Trevor had just handed him the lost Ark of the Covenant.

"Don't make me smack you, boy," Garner muttered.

"There," Trevor said happily. "You share. Consider yourself sworn in, boy. And by the way, King, I'm going with you."

Disgusted, Garner picked up his parcels again. He turned toward Trevor. "You beat everything, you know that? Just everything."

"Thank you kindly, King," Trevor replied before he threw an arm around Hobie's shoulders. "Hobie, did I ever tell you about the time I tracked the murderous Lorne Jessup and his cutthroat gang through the Grand Canyon and nearly got ate by a puma?"

Hobie shook his head, bug-eyed.

"Aw, crud," muttered Garner, and walked away, up the street.

4

This was a fine kettle of fish, Garner thought as he packed up his saddlebags the next morning. Here he had set out alone, on a kind of mission. A drunken mission, but a mission nonetheless, and it was a one-man job. Now he was saddled not only with Hobie Hobson, but with Marcus Trevor too!

That really took the cake, didn't it? The great King Garner being bamboozled by a wet-behind-the-ears lawman. Well, maybe those ears weren't so wet. He'd never ridden with Marcus, but he'd heard tell that he was a decent lawman. Have to be, to get that U.S. deputy marshal's badge. Have to be, for Holling Eberhart to pin it on him. Garner put a lot of faith in Holling.

Course, he'd heard that Trevor was a bit of a showboat, too. A real publicity hound.

Garner didn't care for that part, but he supposed it couldn't be helped. It just went with the territory for most of these federal types.

And he reminded himself that if things had gone just a little differently for him a few years back, Trevor might be dogging *his* trail instead of riding beside him. Garner had seen his share of law troubles way back when, but had come to rest soundly on the side of the law when the citizens of Medicine Rock, Arizona, had talked him into wearing a badge and bringing in Greeley Fox and his boys.

He'd stayed on as law officer in Medicine Rock for seven years, until they decided they needed a new kind of sheriff, one with spit-polished boots and a shiny new suit.

Course, eight months after his "retirement" he'd heard that the Farley brothers had robbed the Medicine Rock bank, and while they were at it, they'd plugged that fancy new sheriff square in the head and killed two others besides.

Garner had done what he supposed was the right thing, although it was against his better instincts. He'd ridden down the Farley brothers. He'd shot it out with them and taken them back to Medicine Rock, draped over their saddles like sacks of feed and smelling to high heaven. He'd thrown their reins over the rail, dropped the bag of bank money smack at Mayor Hodge's feet, then reined his horse around and ridden out of town, all without saying a word.

He'd been that mad at the town, that mad at himself, and that mad at life in general.

Mostly mad at himself, though, because he gave enough of a damn, despite everything, to go out after those pig-nosed, scum-sucking Farleys in the first place.

Of course, this only added to his reputation. The strong, silent, and deadly type, they called him.

Idiots.

He gathered up his belongings, left the room, and pounded on Hobie's door. "Hurry up, dammit," he called. "Daylight's wasting."

"Comin', Boss." The door banged open to reveal Hobie, laden with the pack rig plus his own saddlebags and wearing an ear-to-ear grin. He must have stayed up half the night polishing that silver badge, because the shine on it near about put Garner's eyes out.

Hobie stepped out into the hall, peering first one way, then the other. "Where's Deputy Trevor?"

"Let's light a fire under it, Hobie," Garner said without answering, and started down the hall toward the stairs.

Marcus Trevor was a busy man.

First, he'd gotten up at dawn and sent a wire to U.S. Marshal Holling Eberhart, advising him that he had picked up the best tracker in the Territory, and was hot on Belasco's trail. He didn't mention Garner's name. After all, Eberhart hadn't mentioned it when Trevor talked him into giving him this assignment. Garner had been Trevor's idea, despite any impression that Garner may have been under. And there was no sense in giving old Garner any more credit that he'd have to, when it was over. And besides, he rationalized, Garner really didn't want any credit, now did he?

He grabbed a quick breakfast at Leona's Tasty Café, made a side trip to Atkin's General Store to pick up the supplies he'd ordered yesterday, then popped into the smoke shop down the street for a new pouch of fine-cut tobacco. He made it to the livery before seven, saddled Stealth and Faro and Fly, and then stepped outside and lit a smoke.

Oh, King Garner had taken the bait, all right, hook, line, and sinker! Trevor grinned around his cigarette. God bless drunkards, he thought, because they don't think too straight.

If Garner had been a sober man the day Trevor rode into his ranch, the cranky old bird never would have fallen for it, not in a million years.

"Here's to whiskey," he said softly.

He settled back against the livery wall and got comfortable.

Unfortunately, Marcus Trevor was waiting for them at the livery, which dashed Garner's hopes of getting out of Phoenix without him. Bad enough to take on another man. Worse, when that man suddenly outranked you. And was more than fifteen years your junior.

"Been waitin' long, Deputy?" Hobie asked brightly, and put down the pack rig, along with his share of the foodstuffs he and Garner had just picked up at the mercantile.

Trevor nodded. "Since five," he lied. "Mornin', King. Or should I say good afternoon?"

"Funny as a crutch, Marcus," Garner replied.

He gladly dumped his half of the supplies at Hobie's feet, then walked on into the livery. It was only a quarter to eight, but Trevor had been there a spell, all right, because Faro and Fly were already saddled. He led them both outside, and tethered them on the fence. The trader had brought down the blue roan mule, too, and Garner instructed Hobie to get the rig on him and start loading their supplies.

Trevor lazed back against the corral and solemnly regarded Garner. "King, you'll pardon me for sayin' it, but you don't look happy."

"You'd better know that I don't take orders, Marcus," Garner said gruffly, "not from you, not from anybody." And then he shouted, "Get that goddamn load balanced!" at Hobie. "You want to ruin that mule before we even get started?"

"Just good at givin' 'em," Trevor said.

Garner nodded. "'Bout the size of it. And why the hell don't you cut that mop off?" he asked suddenly, pointing at Trevor's curls.

"Fine," said Trevor. "Now you're mad at my hair?"

Garner grunted. "I'm pissed off at everything, lately."

Trevor thumbed back the brim of his hat. "Hell, I never would have knowed it, King, but I'm glad to hear it ain't just me. Now, the reason I don't cut my hair is 'cause my wife likes it. And I do too, come to think of it. And the reason I'm ridin' with you—and did I tell you how much I 'preciate it?—is that there's something we haven't let slip to the papers as yet."

Garner cocked a brow. "And that's what?"

"Donny Belasco picked himself up a sidekick."

Garner scowled. "You're crazy as Belasco. He works alone. The sick ones like that always do."

Trevor shook his head. "This time, he's partnered up. Found somebody who likes to watch, I guess, and who likes a little fun on the side. You're gonna be real interested in who it is."

"Doubt that."

"Haven't told you yet," Trevor said, rolling himself a smoke. "It's Vince Martindale."

Well, Trevor had Garner's attention now, that was for certain.

Garner scowled. He said, "I thought they hanged that skunk over in New Mexico two years ago."

Trevor said, "I thought so too." He lit the smoke, then

shook out the sulphur tip. "Turns out the feller they hanged was the wrong one. Kept on swearin' it on stacks of Bibles and his mama's grave, but they hanged him anyway." He blew out a yellowish plume and shrugged. "Anybody can make a mistake, I reckon."

"Some mistake."

"Hey, Boss?" Hobie interrupted. "Where'd you put them parcels you brung from the hotel?"

Without looking at him, Garner pointed and said, "Right under your nose."

"Okay," said Hobie, then paused. "Who's Vince Martindale?"

Now Garner turned toward him. "You been living in a tree, boy?"

"No," Hobie said a little indignantly. "I been livin' on a horse ranch where nobody reads the papers or talks about anything 'cept which mare is due to foal next. Who is he, Deputy?"

Trevor tugged at his earlobe, then blew out a thin stream of smoke. "You ever hear of the Elbow Ridge Massacre?"

Hobie went pale. "Yeah, sure," he answered. "It happened when I was a kid, maybe sixteen or so."

"Your daddy tell you what happened?" Trevor asked.

"Why don't you go on back home, Hobie?" King interrupted almost kindly. "Jim and Fred'll be eating up all your good canned goods for sure."

But Hobie was riveted on Trevor. He swallowed hard and said, "Folks said somebody set fire to a bunch of Mexicans. While they was alive. Said they tried to make it look like Apaches had done it."

Trevor grunted. "We didn't buy that for a slap second. Hell, the Apaches were on the reservation then, had been for years, and none of 'em was escaped at the moment." He took a breath. "Three Mexican families were on their way to Ehrenberg. Tied 'em to their wagon wheels and dumped kerosene on 'em. Men, women, even little kids. Vince Martindale was one'a the animals responsible. More than that, he was the ringleader. That boy's just plain mean, through and through."

Garner stared off into the distance, his eyes focused on a rooftop past the corral. There was evil in the world, just as surely as there was good.

"That ranch wife Donny Belasco killed?" Trevor went on. "What they didn't put in the papers was that her husband was killed, too. Poor sonofabitch was locked up in his own outhouse and burnt alive."

At last, Garner looked back at Trevor. "But nobody got burned to death in Tucson. Did they?"

"Not exactly."

"Then how do you know Vince Martindale's still with him?"

Trevor sighed. "That drunk in the alley, the one Donny Belasco tripped over after he sliced up the girl? Somebody doused him with kerosene and tossed a match. A couple of passersby, just leavin' the saloon at closing, got to him in time. He'll live. But he ain't gonna be pretty."

Deep in the wild Sonoran Desert of southern Arizona, Donny Belasco had just finished shaving. He'd been up for hours, but he was just getting around to the finer things in life. He wiped his chin and cheeks carefully with a rag, cleaned his long razor—always sharp and shiny—and folded it, then tucked it into his saddlebags along with his mirror.

Humming, he poured himself a fresh cup of coffee. "Wake up, Martindale," he said for the third time.

Martindale mumbled something abysmally coarse, and rolled over again.

Donny shrugged and leaned back against a boulder. He did make awfully good coffee, if he said so himself. It was the scrape of nutmeg that did it.

"Martindale?" he said again, in a voice light and pleasant. "I'm only going to cook breakfast once. Those who snooze through it will go hungry till lunch. And I have a big morning planned."

Martindale groaned and rolled toward him. He was a middle-sized, middle-aged man, with dark, shaggy hair and deep-set brown eyes, and his face hadn't had a close relationship with a razor in a good two weeks. Maybe three.

Probably just as well, Donny idly mused as he studied Martindale over the rim of his cup. That way, the stubble nearly covered up his old burn scars. They did rather put a fellow off his feed.

Now, Donny himself was a wholly different matter, tonsorially speaking. He was proud of the color of his reddish hair—not too light, not too dark, but a gentle copper color in the sun—and he kept it (and the matching mustache) neatly trimmed.

Of course, this hadn't been the case while he was in residence at Yuma Prison. That philistine of a barber never could get it right, and the powers that be refused to give Donny access to a pair of scissors, even for a moment, to cut it himself.

Barbarians.

Donny was a few inches taller than Martindale at nearly six feet in his boots and socks, with a trim figure and a very young face. Not quite so baby-faced anymore, though, he reminded himself. Prison life had worn away the soft, fatty roundness and given him a slightly harder look. But not too hard. And toiling in the sun had given his skin a lovely coppery glow instead of the pale and pasty look he used to favor.

He was still, he thought, an incredibly attractive man for somebody who'd hit the advanced age of thirty-three.

Why, he didn't look a day past twenty-five!

"Vince, darling?" he said gently.

"Gettin' up, goddamn it," Martindale grumbled from his pallet, although he didn't open his eyes. "Quit naggin'. And quit callin' me darlin' or I'll punch your damn nose out the back of your skull."

"I took a little ride this morning while you were still in the arms of Morpheus," Donny offered, cheerfully ignoring Martindale's threat. He put down his cup and began to get things ready for breakfast.

There was bacon and a pan to fry it in, and the fixings for biscuits. Not fancy, but any food in the free and open air was miles better than the most elegant prison repast. Not that cornmeal mush and fatback or thin, watery bean soup—which Frankie Garza, the head cook, had undoubtedly pissed in—was precisely elegant.

Donny set the pan with the bacon on the fire, and mixed up the batter for the biscuits. "I found a little ranch about five miles south," he continued in a conversational tone. "Just one man and his young wife, it appears. Well, and a hired hand. Anyway, someone was sleeping in the barn."

Martindale opened an eye. "How'd you know he were sleepin' in the barn? Did you ride on in?"

Donny closed his eyes for a moment, then patiently

said, "No, Vincent. I saw him come out of the barn and go into the outhouse."

"Oh."

"He's Mexican. Don't you have a special affinity for Mexicans?"

Vince's brow furrowed, and Donny added, "That is to say, don't you prefer them?"

Martindale scowled. "Goddamn Meskins," he grumbled.

"She's pretty enough, from what I could tell through the spyglass," Donny said wistfully. "The wife, I mean." He spooned the biscuits—loose, only vaguely doughy blobs made without anything so fancy as baking powder—into the hot bacon grease, where they immediately started to sizzle and spread.

"You makin' them friggin' fried things again?" Martindale grumbled. He pulled himself up on one elbow, then sat all the way up and yawned, wide, yellow teeth catching the light. Fumes came in foggy clouds from his mouth, like vapor in the winter. "Don't know how you got the nerve to call 'em biscuits."

"One makes do," replied Donny, trying not to look. Martindale's teeth reminded him of a poorly made and neglected picket fence. Neglected, that is, except by every male dog in the neighborhood. And his breath was caustic enough to peel the hide off a buffalo.

Martindale rubbed grubby fists into his eyes, let out a tremendous fart, then sighed. "When we goin' in?"

"After breakfast."

5

Hobie was still arguing with himself by the time they were most of the way down to Tucson.

It had been different, somehow, when they just were after Donny Belasco. Donny only killed girls, after all. It had seemed Hobie was riding off to save those women, Belasco's future victims, kind of like an old time knight on a quest. Except he'd been secure in the knowledge that he wouldn't be harmed himself.

Now he knew in his heart that this kind of thinking was wrong-headed. Hadn't Donny Belasco cornered Garner into a gunfight just before he was arrested? At least, that was what U.S. Deputy Marshal Trevor had told Hobie. But somehow, Hobie felt like it wasn't going to happen to him. Trevor was there, and Garner was there—and Hobie? He was just going to be the witness.

But Vince Martindale? That was another matter. This one was a killer with no prejudice whatsoever. Oh, he preferred torturing Mexicans, for what reason Hobie couldn't fathom, but he killed men, women, and children of all nationalities, and he burned them alive.

Another shudder ran through Hobie, and he was glad he was riding last in line so that no one could see.

Burning. There were a lot of ways for a man to die, but he figured burning to be the worst. With water, you just slipped away, he figured, just kind of choked a little and that was it. If you got shot, you either died or you didn't. Knife, the same thing. But fire?

The only thing that had kept him from turning tail right there in that Phoenix livery yard was what Garner would think of him for it, right at the moment and forever after. He sure didn't want Garner thinking less of him, even if the man kept it to himself, even if he never said a damned thing.

Hobie would know it, and that was enough.

At least he figured to be in good company. In fact, he couldn't think of better, if a fellow was dumb enough to be going on a manhunt for a couple of mad-dog crazy killers.

That's how Hobie was thinking of himself these past few days. Dumb with a capital D. He figured that back home, Jim and Fred had pigged their way through at least half his larder. He got mad, just thinking about it.

They'd best not be neglecting the horses, that was all he had to say! Garner would be hell to live with for the next year if they'd forgotten to feed, just once—and Garner would know it somehow, too—or failed to have those new foals halter-broke by the time he got back.

If we get back at all, Hobie thought dismally. The last night or so, he'd been imagining his body sent home in an urn, all mixed up with the remnants of a charred outhouse. Maybe some joker would toss the blackened hasp in there with him.

Real dad-gum funny.

He caught himself being mad at some man he didn't know for doing something he hadn't even though of yet, and rolled his eyes.

"Hobie!" shouted Garner.

Hobie clucked to the trailing Charlie Blue, then nudged Fly into a trot. He rode past the deputy and up even with Garner. "Yeah, Boss?" he said, quickly moving his boot out of the path of Charlie Blue's big old yellow teeth. The mule had turned out to be a nipper. "What you need?"

Garner tipped his head. "You see that hunk of rock up ahead?"

It was the first actual landmark they'd come upon since leaving Phoenix behind, this stretch of territory being the most godforsaken piece of land in the whole U.S. of A. At least, that was the Gospel according to Hobie.

Hobie nodded. "You bet. I seen it since it was just a bump on the ground." Right now, it was beginning to jut up against the sky.

"Well, that's Picacho Peak," Garner said. "Tucson isn't far past, so you can quite bitchin' about the landscape."

Hobie didn't say anything, as he'd been complaining a good bit about the dreariness of the ride.

He'd also been waiting for somebody to do something heroic. So far, the closest he'd got to this was Marcus Trevor's bragging, and he was beginning to get the feeling that near all of it was stretched near to breaking.

"Only battle of the Civil War fought in Arizona was

fought right there," said Trevor, who had ridden up beside them. "Believe Jack Swilling was in on that. Hey!" he shouted, suddenly reining his horse to the side. "Watch that damn mule!"

Hobie yanked on Charlie Blue's lead rope, effectively pulling him out of range. Charlie Blue was not amused, and clicked his teeth a couple of times on the air.

Garner grumbled something under his breath, but Hobie was fairly certain it didn't have anything to do with the mule. Garner looked as if he didn't approve one bit of Jack Swilling, whoever he was. Hobie wasn't inclined to ask.

But Trevor was in a talkative mood, and said, "You ever hear of ol' Jack Swilling, Hobie?"

"Can't say as I have," he replied.

Trevor put one hand on his saddle horn and leaned back. "Confederate officer. After the war, he rode on up to Phoenix and found the old canals."

"Got drunk and tripped into one, more like," Garner muttered.

Trevor ignored him. "You remember those irrigation canals, don't you, Hobie?"

Hobie shrugged. "I thought somebody just dug some ditches."

"Sorta," Trevor went on with a grin. "Way back in the olden days, there was a tribe of Indians—the Hohokam—who lived there and dug 'em. The Hohokam are all gone now. Nobody knows where they went off to. But they left them canals. Anyhow, Swilling found 'em and cleared 'em out—"

"More like he oversaw that Indian he used to ride around with," Garner interrupted grumpily. "Probably sat around in the shade, barkin' orders and guzzling poppy juice and—"

Trevor twisted in his saddle. "You gonna let me tell this, King?"

Garner raised a hand and looked away.

"As a matter of fact," Trevor said to Hobie, twisting back, "I heard he did used to ride with an Indian, name of Tonto. Always thought it was right peculiar, that Indian taking that name, since it means stupid. But what the hell, right?"

Hobie nodded.

"Anyhow, once he got those ditches free of brush and the like, he started talkin' up the place. He called it Pumpkinville, mostly, 'cause they was so many wild ones growin' in the valley. Course, folks changed it to Phoenix. Don't rightly know when that happened."

Garner turned toward them. "If you're gonna tell some pointless story that happened when you were still wearing diapers, at least tell it right, Marcus."

Trevor tucked his chin indignantly. "Why, I thought I was, there, King!"

Garner rolled his eyes. "It was like this, Hobie. Swilling was an old drunk, and he was real fond of opium, too. Drank laudanum by the gallon and used an old war wound for an excuse. He fell in one of those canals by accident, then tried to bamboozle the populace at large into movin' to his irrigated land. He named the place Pumpkinville, all right, but another drunkard named Darrel Duppa changed it to Phoenix. Some crud about how the phoenix bird rose up out of the ashes, and how a city was gonna rise up after the Hohokam. He was loony, if you ask me. Nothin's ever gonna come of Phoenix."

Hobie didn't rightly agree, but he kept his opinion to himself. Garner looked to be right on the edge.

But Trevor tugged thoughtfully at his mustache. "Oh, yeah. Duppa. Now I remember. Weren't he an English lord or somethin'?"

"Only drunk as one," Garner replied nastily. "Why, he walked out of the ramada where the so-called city fathers were having their big meeting, and stood looking across the Rio Salado at this scruffy little Mexican settlement—they used to call it Santa Rosa or somethin' like that. Well, he babbled in Italian or French or Russian, for all I know, for a spell with his arms all spread out, like he was orating on some stage. Then he switched back to American and said he'd decided that it reminded him of the 'verdant vales of Tempe.' Christ on a crutch! Poor Mexicans got stuck with it, too. Tempe, that is."

"Was that over where they had that ferry and the mill on the other side of the river?" Hobie asked, thinking to defuse the situation.

Both Trevor and Garner ignored him. He'd expected as much.

Trevor shook his head. "Now, who the hell told you that?"

"Nobody," growled Garner. "I was there when they had that meeting. The whole batch of 'em were sozzled out of their minds."

"King," said Trevor, "I'm thinkin' you're awful hard of late on those who pour the bug juice now and then. Wouldn't have anything to do with—"

"Shut up, Marcus," Garner snapped, and pushed Faro into a jog.

•   •   •

They arrived in Tucson that evening, and took rooms at the Cactus Wren Hotel. Hobie appeared to be more than a little fascinated by the running water in the bathroom, and just sat there, turning the tap on, then off; on, then off.

Garner and Trevor, however, hiked over to the sheriff's office and introduced themselves to the short, portly, gravelly voiced sheriff, whose name was Parker Duffy.

"*The* King Garner?" rumbled Duffy, his brows arched. "Pardon me all to hell, but I thought you was dead!"

"Only feel like it," replied Garner.

"King, here, volunteered to come out of retirement to help me track down Donny Belasco, ain't you, King?" Trevor said brightly.

"You was retired?" asked Duffy.

"I raise horses, damn it," barked Garner. "Donny Belasco. Which way'd he head?"

The sheriff folded his arms and scowled. "Well, now, if I was privy to that bit of information, you think I'd be standing here chewin' the fat with you raggedy boys? He's just gone, that's all. Reckon you'll have to wait for a new victim to turn up 'fore you find out where he went off to."

Then the sheriff leaned close and glanced at the front door, then the front windows. "You fellers know he ain't alone, don't you?"

"Heard about your burnin'," Trevor replied. "Can we talk to the man?"

Duffy worked his mouth to one side. "You can, for all the good it'll do you. Jake don't remember much except Donny Belasco's face. Said when Donny tripped over him, Donny went ass-over-teakettle. Next thing Jake knew, somebody was sloppin' kerosene, and it weren't Donny."

"Maybe he heard something," offered Garner.

"Nope," said Duffy. "I asked. But go ahead and ask him again if'n you want. Where you boys stayin', in case I get word?"

"The Cactus Wren," said Trevor. "You wouldn't know where I could find a newspaper, would you?"

Garner and Trevor were unable to get anything more out of Jake Farrow, Vince Martindale's latest victim, than Sheriff Duffy had. Garner wasn't surprised. When a man was as drunk as Jake Farrow had been, it was a miracle that he remembered so much as Donny Belasco's face. He'd told them, through layers of bandages, that he remembered it because he'd never seen a prettier man look uglier than Donny did when he hit the dirt.

So Garner and Trevor went back to the hotel, collected Hobie, and had a good steak dinner at the Blue Heron restaurant. It had been there the last time Garner was through Tucson and the meat was still as choice, cooked just to order—Garner liked his bloody—and served with all the trimmings and some besides. He knew for a fact that some places down here dragged in anything that died on the street, whether it be bovine, equine, or canine, burnt the holy hell out of it, and served it as beef. He didn't figure Hobie was quite up to that yet.

Come to think of it, he wasn't either.

After supper, they repaired to the Silver Spur Saloon, where Trevor had a couple of shots, Hobie nursed a beer, and Garner stared at one while he rolled and smoked four cigarettes. He wasn't ready to try another drink just yet.

Besides, what Trevor had said back there on the trail—that thing about him being touchy about the subject of boozers—still rankled him, mostly because it was true.

Afterwards, Garner broke off from the others and found himself a woman. She was dark, her name was Carlita, she had clean room at a cheap hotel on the other side of town, and he supposed that if he'd seen her face in the daylight it might have scared him. But it had been a long time for him, after all, and she only charged two bits.

He ended up spending four.

After Garner's defection, Marcus Trevor walked back up to the hotel with Hobie. "You go on up, boy," he said, settling into one of the two battered leather chairs in the lobby. "I'm gonna sit and have me a smoke and read the paper before I turn in."

Hobie made some sounds like maybe he'd stay, too, but Trevor intimated that he wanted to be alone. To consider the case, he said.

He waited a few minutes after Hobie had gone up to his room, then tucked the paper under his arm. He sidled up to the desk clerk and showed him his badge.

"You know where this fella lives?" he whispered, pointing at the byline on a particularly lurid story about the murdered prostitute. "Official business."

The desk clerk gulped and practically tripped over himself, he gave that address so fast.

"Don't mention this to anyone," Trevor cautioned. "Not even the fellers I rode in with, not the sheriff, not nobody. Got that?"

With the clerk nodding nervously behind him, Trevor turned and went out the door.

While Hobie and Garner and Trevor were at breakfast the next morning—and Garner was uncomfortably taking a good-natured razzing for disappearing the night before—Sheriff Duffy walked in.

He came over to the table, spurs clanking, and said, "Mornin', boys," without an ounce of pleasantness on his face. "Mind?" he asked, and pulled up a chair.

"Too late if I did," said Trevor.

Garner was more to the point. "Another killing?" he asked.

The sheriff tipped his head toward Hobie, who was presently engaged with a thick stack of pancakes. "He all right?"

"He's my other deputy," said Trevor, and Garner ground his teeth.

Sheriff Duffy leaned in, and gestured for them to do the same. "They went down to Baker. Just outside of it anyhow. Man and his wife—Ezra and Annie Cartwell—was found dead yesterday. She'd been all cut up, and he'd been burnt to death in his barn. There was a hired man, name of Ramon Diaz. Identified Belasco and Martindale from the posters."

"H-how'd this Ramon Diaz get through it?" asked Hobie, his pancakes forgotten. His napkin was tightly caught up in his fists, the knuckles of which were white and bloodless.

"Martindale didn't toss him in the barn with his boss," Duffy whispered, sliding his eyes from side to side. "Said that after he'd been hog-tied and listenin' to Ezra scream for while, Martindale doused him with coal oil and dragged him over to a shed. Threw him in it, set him afire, then locked the door."

There was a sick, tearing sound, and Garner looked over to see that Hobie's napkin was half ripped apart.

"Easy, boy, easy," Garner murmured, like he was talking to a nervous horse.

"What Martindale didn't realize," Sheriff Duffy continued in a low voice, "was that what he'd throwed Diaz into was the pump shed. Diaz said he managed to knock the lid off the well and threw hisself down it. But by that time, his clothes had pretty well lit the shed, so Martindale was none the wiser."

Garner pushed his eggs away. How long, he wondered, had Ramon Diaz been down that well, his hands tied, and all burnt? He noticed that the news hadn't hurt Trevor's appetite, though. He was practically scraping the pattern off his plate.

"When?" Garner asked.

"Found 'em last night," Duffy said. "Just got the wire."

"No," Garner growled. "When did it happen?"

"Oh," Duffy said, and leaned back in his chair. "Two days ago, give or take."

Garner scraped back his chair. "Hobie?" he said, and the boy stood right up. He was wobbling a little and white as a sheet, but he stood. Next, Garner looked at Marcus Trevor, who was drinking the last of his coffee. "Well?" Garner said. "You gonna sit there all damn day feeding your face? Let's get moving."

Trevor stood up, pulled the checkered napkin out of his collar, and dropped it on the table. "Ain't gotta ask me twice."

Garner was two steps from the door, with Trevor and

Hobie close on his heels, when a young man entered from outside and nearly ran into him.

He was short, not as short as Hobie but close to it, wore a pair of gold-rimmed spectacles that had slithered halfway down his nose, and was dressed like a back-Easter, in a gray suit and a short-brimmed hat.

"King Garner!" he exclaimed brightly. "What luck! Just the man I wanted to see!"

"You've seen me," Garner growled, and went to move him aside.

But the man ducked away and said, "You don't understand, Mr. Garner. My name's Clive Woolsey. *Tucson Herald.*" He pulled a small pad and the stub of a yellow pencil from his coat pocket. "Is it true that you're out after the fiends Belasco and Martindale?" he asked, pencil poised.

6

"I'm real sorry, fellers," said Sheriff Duffy, pushing in between Garner and the reporter. "Dammit, Clive, go back to the newspaper office and drink some ink or somethin'. This ain't none of your business."

"Oh, but it is, it is!" said Woolsey, pushing his glasses up. "My story about Martindale and the burning of Jake Farrow just hit the streets in the morning edition. It was a genuine scoop! Sheriff Duffy, you really should confide in me about these things. I'm afraid I didn't paint you in the kindest—"

Marcus Trevor pushed past Garner and grabbed Woolsey by his collar. "Keep your damned voice down!" he hissed, and hauled him outside.

Garner went out after him, as did the others. "Little late for that, isn't it, Marcus?" he asked rhetorically.

"How'd you find out about Martindale, you little sheep turd?" Trevor hissed, once he had Woolsey pressed up against the clapboards.

"Yeah," added Sheriff Duffy, rather ineffectually.

Woolsey wriggled uncomfortably, but he managed to arch one pale brow. "I have my sources, and I don't have to divulge them to you. Or anyone, for that matter. You can't really expect that someone could attempt to immolate a human being right in the center of town, and that no one would find out about it, Duffy. Even if it did happen on the heels of that girl's horrible death, and even if it did happen in the middle of the night."

Woolsey stared at the deputy for a second, then added, "You must be Marcus Trevor. I should have known you by your hair. It's quite famous, you know. Samson-esque, quite Samson-esque! Are you going to hold me here until my suit rips?"

Grudgingly, Trevor let him down, and Woolsey made a show of smoothing his hair and jacket and straightening his spectacles. "A sterling choice," Woolsey said, wiping imaginary dust from his sleeve. "A wise decision. I wield a rather important pen in this community, if I do say so myself."

"You won't when it's shoved up your ass," muttered Garner, and behind him, he heard Hobie titter. He said, "C'mon, Marcus. What's done is done. Hobie, you come on, too." He turned back toward their hotel.

Garner smiled wide for the first time in days. As much as he disliked Woolsey, it actually amused him to see Trevor's applecart dumped like that.

As he marched up the boardwalk, he was thinking that it would take him all of five minutes to gather his things. Another ten minutes to get the horses tacked up and ready, and then they could start for Baker. Belasco and Martindale's track would be a few days old, but some sign might still be there. And he realized that he was counting on Hobie as much as himself to ferret it out.

Behind him, he heard that damned reporter still pestering Marcus Trevor with questions, and he just walked faster. Let Trevor deal with it.

Except, once they gained the hotel lobby, Hobie reminded him that he had to stop and refresh their supply of foodstuffs, and Trevor, who walked in a few seconds later, announced—far too joyously—that Woolsey would be going with them.

"What the hell happened?" Garner fairly shouted. First the supplies, and now this! "Two minutes ago you were ready to snap that little bastard's head off." He ground his teeth. "Bad enough that I've got to take you and Hobie along."

"*You've* got to take us?" Trevor asked, eyebrows hiked.

Garner ignored him. "And now you're telling me that I've got to put up with some slicker of a scribbler, too! He's gonna slow us up, Marcus. You know that. And what if he gets sliced to pieces? Or turned into barbecue?"

"I shall take my chances, Mr. Garner," said Woolsey, who had popped his head in the door. "No risk is too great for this lowly reporter when the people need to know."

King took an angry step toward him, but Trevor pulled him back. Woolsey ducked outside again.

"He's got a point, there, King," Trevor said soothingly.

"Sure," Garner snapped. "On the top of his head. And I'm about to pound it flat for him. Dammit, Marcus, who's gonna hitch their wagon to us next? A brass marchin' band?"

"He says the public has a right to know, Boss," Hobie offered meekly.

"Sure," snapped Garner. "Side with him." He jerked his thumb toward Trevor and nearly put the man's eye out.

"I ain't sidin' with anybody!" Hobie cried, and took a step backwards, smack into one of the leather armchairs. He fell into the seat in a tangled heap, one leg dangling over an arm.

"That's right, King," Trevor said quickly. "After all, he's already broke the news about Martindale bein' along with Donny Belasco. It's already hit the streets. He can't do any more damage. And, well, politically speakin' . . ."

"Stop right there," Garner cut in, mad as a wet cat. "If you're gonna tell me that this is just one big step in your stinkin' career—"

"Cut it out!" cried Hobie, and Garner realized that not only was the kid back on his feet, but he'd planted himself between Garner and Trevor.

"Don't go bein' mad at each other!" Hobie shouted. "I been pretty damned scared ever since I heard that we was goin' after a man-burner. I don't mind fessin' up to that. But while we were comin' up here, while you fellers were gettin' ready to rip each other's heads off, I been thinking about how everybody's goin' after these boys for his own selfish reasons."

Garner blinked, and Trevor took a step back, brows lifted in umbrage.

"Selfish?" Trevor said. "Never heard nothin' so peculiar. It's my job, boy!"

"You're crazy, Hobie," Garner said, although he said it with less conviction that he might have.

"No, sir, I'm not," Hobie said firmly. "You," he said,

jabbing a finger toward Trevor, "are doin' it 'cause you figure to get a big raise, or maybe you figure to move up from U.S. deputy marshal to just plain U.S. marshal, or maybe you figure to get more famous. You know, the . . . the dazzle of it. And you, Boss," he said, shifting the accusing finger toward Garner, "figure that it's some big responsibility of yours. Like you're the one who let Donny Belasco bust out, personal-like, and you're the only one what can put him back in jail. Or mayhap finish him for good, this time."

Garner couldn't think of a damned thing to say.

Hobie took a breath. "And the both of you, somewhere inside, figure to have a big adventure out of it."

"A goddamn adventure?" sneered Trevor. "Hobie, I think you're drinkin' all of that booze King's leavin' alone."

"And me?" Hobie went on, oblivious. "I guess I just wanted to see somebody be a real hero while there was still time. Mayhap even get to be a little bit of a hero myself."

Angrily, Trevor said, "What you mean, while there's still time?"

Hobie shrugged. "Before everything gets too . . . too new, I guess."

Slowly, Garner shook his head. "Hobie, I swear, I don't have the least idea what floats around inside your brain."

Trevor folded his arms. "Me neither," he sniffed.

Hobie sighed. "I'm just sayin' that if this reporter wants to come along, well, we should just let him. It might be his last chance, too. You know?"

"Well, Mr. Garner?" said Woolsey, who had somehow snuck back into the lobby while they were busy arguing. "What's the consensus? I warn you that if you say no, I shall simply ride a hundred yards behind you. I'm not proud. I just want my story. I also remind you that U.S. Deputy Marshal Trevor is in charge of the case, and he has already given me permission to accompany you. I should hate to exclude a man like you, Mr. Garner, from this story. Or paint you as a shirker."

Garner glared at Trevor, who just shrugged.

"Jesus," Garner muttered. Still shaking his head, he simply turned and started up the stairs.

Behind him, he heard Trevor say, "Believe that's a yes, there, Woolsey."

"Splendid!" Woolsey replied. "I'll meet you at Woodson's Livery in three shakes!"

Several hours later, Hobie didn't know what to make of Clive Woolsey.

Sure, Hobie had stood up for the reporter back in Tucson. He'd even surprised himself with that, and had had to sit down and think how to breathe once he got back up to his room.

Geez Louise!

But once he'd recovered his composure—and realized he'd emerged mercifully unmurdered by Garner—he'd felt oddly peaceful.

Not for long, though.

There was Woolsey.

He supposed Woolsey was a likable enough fellow. He was a lot closer to Hobie's height, for one thing, which meant Hobie didn't get a crick in his neck just talking to him. He was yellow-headed, too, although not so fair as Hobie with his wavy hair, which was so light to begin with that in summer it went to white. Woolsey's hair was dead straight, and he wore it parted in the middle and cut straight across, real neat, right at the level of his chin and tucked behind his ears.

He talked a little funny, too, but Hobie didn't hold that against him. Woolsey had said he was originally from Rhode Island, and Hobie supposed that it was just how Rhode Island people talked.

He was also a lot closer to Hobie's age, being (he had confided) twenty-four.

None of these things much concerned Hobie one way or the other, other than to note them.

What he did think was odd was that Woolsey had wanted to come along in the first place—had chanced getting himself knocked to kingdom come to do it, too. But once he'd lived through that part and they'd actually gotten going, he'd stopped talking to anyone at all.

Now, Hobie had always figured that reporters were nosy by nature, and apt to talk and ask questions or at least spout knowledge of one sort or other nonstop. He'd kind of been looking forward to being asked some questions by a smart fellow like Woolsey. Maybe learn something.

After all, back home, Garner hardly ever talked at all except when he was telling somebody what to do, and Jim and Fred weren't worth wasting much breath on. Trevor had talked up a storm so far, but he hardly ever gave anybody else a chance to chime in. Hobie, on the other hand, liked to talk. And he especially wanted somebody to ask him about himself.

Why had Hobie come along with Garner and Trevor in the first place? That was one question Woolsey could have, should have asked. Hobie knew there were lots of others, too, although he couldn't rightly think of them. And he wanted to hear his answers as much as he wanted to be asked the questions.

But no. They'd been on the trail for a half a day already, and Woolsey was just hanging back on that piss-poor black mare he'd rented back in Tucson, his lips pressed together so darn tight they were practically clenched.

There was just no figuring some folks.

Of course, Garner hadn't exactly been the life of the hoe-down, as his mama used to say, since they left Tucson, either. Hobie hadn't expected him to be. He had that kind of half-surly, half-disgusted look on his face, like the time when Fred had left the grain room unlocked and two mares had got in there and about foundered themselves on a buffet of rolled oats.

Oh, Hobie knew that look, and he knew better than to interrupt whatever was going on behind Garner's eyes.

Deputy Trevor had been pretty quiet, too, and he was usually talkative even when there was nothing to talk about. Before he shut up for seemingly good and all, he'd told Hobie that where they were going—that being Baker—was about a day and a half's ride away.

"Probably more like two, what with that damn mule along," Trevor had added, sliding a mean glance at Charlie Blue.

Hobie knew it wasn't the mule. He figured it was because they were four people now instead of three, and Trevor was having second thoughts about letting Woolsey tag along. It was too late, though.

Hobie twisted in his saddle to make sure that Woolsey was still back there.

Yup. He was.

Although at the moment, he sure looked a lot like Hobie's daddy had when his piles were pestering him.

•   •   •

Clive Woolsey saw Hobie look back. He affected a careless expression—or one which he hope conveyed that emotion—and tried not to bounce.

He hated this horse. He hated the dust and the grime and the heat. Basically, he hated the out-of-doors, period. The one and only thing that had made him talk his way into the group's good graces—and the one and only thing that had made him listen when Deputy Trevor had come to call the night before—was that if he could get this story, it would absolutely make his career.

A pyromaniac and a lady-killer, both of them of the most murderous and grisly sort imaginable! It would be a genuine coup, something the back-East papers could really sink their fangs into. Why, he'd be eating off this for a good long while, and eating back in Rhode Island, to boot!

Or maybe New York. He hadn't decided yet, although he was inclined toward the latter. Anyplace but here.

He'd come West because he'd lost a bet. Oh, nobody needed to tell him he'd been a fool. He'd realized that the morning after he'd bet Curtis Lassiter that he could drink him under the table—and lost.

So much for college bets, especially the sort you made the night of graduation. Curtis Lassiter took Clive's job on the *Post,* and Clive took Curtis's with the *Tucson Herald.*

He supposed Curtis Lassiter was still laughing up his sleeve.

Well, he'd show them not to discount Clive Woolsey. He'd show them all.

But in the meantime, he was stuck out here on this ridiculous animal following a pack of ridiculous men. Honestly, that hair of Trevor's—talk about an affectation! Last night, while Trevor had given him the scoop on Martindale, he'd kept fussing with it like a girl with her first beau at a church social.

But then, Woolsey supposed he wanted to write about men with outrageous affectations who performed even more outrageous deeds. They made for the best kind of stories, didn't they?

He supposed that he could stand Trevor so long as he got his story.

And then there was Mr. High-and-Mighty King Garner.

Woolsey made a face that had nothing to do with the dust he was continually wiping off his face and glasses.

Garner was supposedly a legend back in the Dark Ages, which was, to Woolsey, anything that had happened more than five years ago. Of course, his editor had repeatedly drilled into him that they weren't after stories about the old days, not about has-beens, that this was the modern age and that they should put Arizona's wild past—her gunmen, both good and bad, and her wild Indians—behind them.

He didn't get any argument from Woolsey.

What Woolsey was supposed to bring in—and what he fully intended to sell to the papers back East, whether his editor at the *Herald* knew it or not—was the thrilling story of the manhunt. There'd be other articles too, about the background of the case and the criminals, and all with as much gruesome detail as possible.

The only one who seemed willing to even speak to him about the case was Trevor, and all Trevor wanted to do—besides yammer endlessly, Woolsey thought with a silent snarl—was get somebody to make him famous.

Oh, Woolsey had brushed shoulders with his like before. They were theatrical in both attitude and appearance. Some wore fringe, some notched their guns, some dressed in black or all in white. They had no problem talking about themselves at great length, and they knew—or thought they knew—just who to cozy up to, and when.

That old bull Garner, on the other hand, would just as soon have slit Woolsey's gullet and left him for dead in a ditch as cozy up to him—if indeed there was such a thing as a ditch out here. Woolsey was fairly convinced that most if not all of Garner's reputation was hearsay, the result of too many free drinks given to too many cowboys who'd known someone's uncle who'd known someone's cousin who'd known someone's friend who'd been there when Garner supposedly performed some deed or other. That usually turned out to be the case with these fellows with big reputations.

And Hobie? Woolsey gave a derisive sniff. Why, Hobie Hobson was little better than comic relief, and not much good at that, either. He wasn't worth the time it would take to ask him to spell his name correctly.

Woolsey pulled a handkerchief from his pocket and ran it around his neck, then over his face. Blasted heat, and it was only May.

Lord save him from spending another summer here!

Donny Belasco and Vince Martindale were feasting on the last of the smoked turkey they'd removed from the home of Ezra and Annie Cartwell. They still had a haunch of smoked pronghorn left, which Donny figured would last them three more days. Two, if Martindale made an animal of himself.

Which he probably would, if he kept true to form.

"Care to pull the wishbone?" Donny said, holding it out.

"Huh?" asked Martindale, and Donny shrugged. Martindale wasn't exactly the sharpest tool in the shed. But then, Donny had known that at the moment he'd run over the top of that ridge outside Yuma, absolutely thrilled just to still be running, and spied Martindale waiting with the horses.

And Martindale had drawn his pistol.

"Who're you?" Martindale had demanded.

Donny had wanted to say something terribly witty, something about being a member of a very fashionable club of gentlemen who wore filthy prison stripes, had bad haircuts, and fastened rusty iron cuffs on their legs just for the sheer amusement of it. But there wasn't time. At any second, the guards were going to come pouring over the ridge after him.

So he'd shouted, "Donny Belasco, you fool!" instead, and vaulted up onto the nearest horse.

"Well, where the hell's Piggy?" Martindale had asked dully.

Piggy, Donny supposed, being "Pignose" Wilcox, who lay somewhere back behind Donny, a rather ugly bullet hole in his back.

Just then, the guards—first one, then another—barreled over the ridge, and Donny had clapped heels to his horse.

With what Donny later discovered was uncharacteristic wisdom, Martindale had decided to save his questions for later.

Donny snapped the wishbone himself, then tried to remember who got his wish—the person with the short end, or the long. Oh, well. He'd won, either way. He tossed the bones over his shoulder, and they clattered lightly to the desert floor.

He thought about it for a moment. "I wish . . . I wish I were in Philadelphia," he muttered. As he recalled, there were plenty of prostitutes in Philadelphia, and more than a few of them were young and pretty.

"Where's that?" Martindale inquired, his mouth full of half-chewed turkey.

"In Pennsylvania," replied Donny. "And didn't anyone ever instruct you not to speak and masticate at the same time?"

A puzzled looked clouded Martindale's features, such as they were, and Donny repeated, "Pennsylvania. It's a state. Back East."

"Oh," said Martindale, and went back to his drumstick.

Really, Donny thought, something had to be done.

He had no stomach for the thing that Martindale loved best. The screams of that farmer had actually bothered him. Ruined all his fun.

Plus, he had concluded that all these burnt edifices, all the smoke rising like a flag that read "Look here!" might just bring the law down that much quicker. He certainly didn't want that.

And he was just plain tired of Martindale. Of all the people to travel with, he had ended up sharing cook fires with an unwashed idiot who had no education, shabby manners, and rather horrid taste in recreation.

Oh, Donny had thought it might be amusing to study another fellow's peccadillos, once he realized who Martindale was. And Martindale was more than eager to renew his habit. It seemed he had abstained for some years, and Donny supposed he had egged him into picking up the brand again. So to speak.

But Martindale was a lout.

He was, in fact, so sloppy in his work that it was a miracle he hadn't been hanged eons ago. Martindale had been more fortunate than he knew to have been jailed for four and a half years in Montana, for petty robbery. It seemed he'd been arrested under another name, and no one had cared enough to bother to ferret out his true identity.

Oh, well. The Lord took care of drunkards and children.

Idiots, too, Donny supposed.

But something would have to be done, he thought as he watched Martindale's filthy hands rip the other drumstick off the carcass.

Something would have to be done.

7

"There it is."

The lawman from Baker, who had introduced himself as Sheriff Hiram H. Watson, pointed ahead to the remains of a small homestead where Ezra and Annie Cartwell, aged twenty-seven and twenty-one respectively, had met their fates.

"Sufferin' Christ Almighty," Trevor muttered, shaking his head in disgust. "Martindale didn't leave so much as a toothpick of that barn standin', did he?"

They rode on down.

The only structure of any note still standing was the house. Even the corrals and the chicken coop, being connected to the barn, had caught fire, leaving only their charred silhouettes on the ground and a few stray chickens idly wandering the premises. The water trough still stood, but only because it had been filled when the fire struck. The side that had been nearest the fence was scorched and blackened, and slowly seeping water.

In the pile of ashes and rubble that had been the barn, a space had been cleared of fallen timbers and debris. There, on what had been the barn's floor, was a grotesque silhouette in reverse: a light and unburnt patch against the fire-scarred floor, a light patch in the distorted and convulsed shape of a man.

In the shape of the late Ezra Cartwell.

The pump house, where the unfortunate Ramon Diaz had jumped down the well, was in ashes, too. Only the scorched, stone ring wall of the well remained, that and a blackened, twisted metal thing that had been the pump. Amazing to think that a man could live through something like that, then survive two days of being stuck down a well.

Of course, Diaz hadn't lived much longer. After they'd hauled him to town, he'd made it a whole day before he found a pistol and somehow managed to fire a bullet into his skull.

"Poor sonofabitch," the doctor had told them, wearily shaking his head. "It was a blessing, though, much as I hate to say it. Diaz didn't have any face left, you know, and only one thumb and two fingers. No matter how much laudanum I gave him, the poor wretch just kept screaming, begging for somebody to end it for him. Finally, he did it himself."

Garner, Hobie, and Sheriff Watson slowly rode on up to the little whitewashed house. Trevor and Woolsey lingered at what was left of the pump house, where Trevor was lengthily expounding on something or other, and Woolsey was frantically—but enthusiastically—scribbling on that damned notepad of his.

The front door of the house stood open, mutely inviting Garner in to see where the carnage had happened, but he hesitated to get off Faro. He was fairly sure of what he was going to find, and he didn't much relish the thought of affirming his suspicions.

Sheriff Watson cleared his throat. "If you don't mind, fellers," he said without looking at anyone or anything but the ground, "I'll just wait for you out here. I don't think I can . . ." The sentence trailed off into nothing, but Garner knew what he meant.

"That's fine," he said, and swung down off Faro. "You stay out here, too, Hobie," he added.

Hobie began, "But—"

"You don't want to see this, boy," Garner said, cutting him off, then added, "I don't want you to see it, either." He handed Faro's reins up to the puzzled boy and walked toward the door.

The house still stank of death, even with the door standing wide. Annie Cartwell had lain there in the heat for days before anybody found her. Garner took a last deep breath of outside air, then went inside.

It was a one-room structure, and Annie Cartwell had been butchered on her bed.

Signs of a struggle—a broken plate, an overturned chair, fallen pictures—were apparent, but few. She'd been small, Sheriff Watson had told him. Easily overpowered.

Blood was spattered halfway up the walls above the bed. It soaked the stiffened sheets and ruined quilt, dotted the floor and braided rug, stained the curtains, even pinked the ceiling here and there in a fine mist.

Garner supposed they'd found a clean dress to bury Annie Cartwell in, because the one she'd been wearing that day was still there, sliced to ribbons by Donny Belasco's razor. Gingerly, he picked it up. It had been cut cleanly down the front, and was dark and stiff with dried blood.

It had once been the color of a robin's egg.

He let the dress fall from his fingers and swallowed, hard. Get a grip on yourself, Garner, he told himself. You've seen all this before. Now, think.

He closed his eyes for a moment.

Donny would have come to the door. "Nice day, ma'am," he would have said. Probably doffed his hat. He would have turned on that charming smile, the one that made all the girls melt and the old women want to bake him cookies. There would have been some excuse, something to get him in the house.

By then, Martindale probably already had the men hog-tied. He would have done that first, and Donny would have helped him. And the door closing behind Donny, that would have been Martindale's signal that he could begin the fun.

Maybe Donny let her listen to her husband pleading for his life before he started on her. Garner hoped not, but what he hoped was neither here nor there. What Donny had done to her, though, that he knew by heart.

The pattern never varied. First, he would have tied her to the bed. Garner could see the marks the ropes had made on the wooden posts, the scars her frantic and terrified struggles had cut into the varnish.

Next came the razor.

First, the ears, both sliced off with surgical precision, and even with the sides of the skull. Next, one slice to each cheek, all the way through the flesh and down to the teeth. That Annie Cartwell had very likely gone into shock long before this happened—probably when Donny showed her the first ear—was of little solace to Garner.

Next, he would have sliced her dress off and pulled it out from under her, discarded it on the floor. At this point, Donny Belasco would have slit her throat. Then, with nearly surgical precision, he would have proceeded to open her up from her ribs to her pubis, and removed her womb and ovaries.

He left the female parts, usually on a plate or a tray placed neatly beside the body. According to Sheriff Watson, Annie's had been left on a piece of Mexican pottery.

Belasco took the ears along. Nobody knew why, and Donny Belasco hadn't enlightened anyone while he was in custody.

While Garner was chasing Donny all those years ago, he'd talked to a couple of doctors. They'd told him that the rest of Donny's handiwork—the gutting part—was post mortem.

"A lack of explosive bleeding," one fellow had called it.

"An absence of spray pattern," another had said.

It didn't matter what they called it. Garner just figured that blood stopped spurting when the heart that had pumped it was mercifully stilled.

But there was still an awful lot of blood, sprayed or seeped, by the time Donny was finished. It had soaked Annie's pretty green quilt—a wedding-ring pattern, he thought they called it, one she'd likely made with her own two hands. It had saturated the straw mattress and pooled beneath the bed into a sticky mess that was still drawing flies days after the fact.

All those years ago at the trial, there had been a great deal of talk. Doctors by the score had testified. Specialists brought in by the defense had said that Donny Belasco was mad as a hatter, said he couldn't be blamed, that he didn't know right from wrong, and that the fact that he always butchered his victims in the same, methodical way was proof of this.

Garner hadn't given a damn about all that claptrap. Still didn't. When somebody was the way Donny Belasco was, you didn't send him off to prison. You didn't lobby for kindness and mercy like the Anti–Capital Punishment League picketers had, and you sure as hell didn't put them in a hospital to study, like the doctors had wanted. You just shot them.

Wouldn't you shoot a mad dog?

Hobie fidgeted in his saddle for a while, then dismounted. He didn't go any closer to the house, though, just stood quietly, holding the horses. Garner had told him to stay put, and besides, he wasn't sure he was ready to see what Garner was in there looking at.

Sheriff Watson stayed in the saddle, though, and brought out a pipe. Nerves, thought Hobie. The man did look kind of pale, and when he held a match to his pipe bowl, his hand shook.

Trevor and a smug-looking Woolsey sauntered up about then, leading their mounts, and without a word handed their reins to Hobie and walked up to the stoop. Which left Hobie not only with a handful of reins, but the mule's lead rope, too.

"The boss says he don't want anybody else in there," Hobie called, for what little good it did. While he fumbled, trying to straighten out the wad of leather and rope, Trevor ushered Woolsey through.

It didn't last long. A few seconds later, Woolsey burst back out like a startled rabbit from its hole, doubled over, and puked all over the front step.

Hobie smiled. Served Woolsey right for all those

I'm-better-than-you looks he'd been tossing around lately.

Trevor, tight-lipped, wasn't far behind. Oh, he didn't puke, but he looked awful white.

"They was warned," muttered Sheriff Watson grimly.

Garner came out a few minutes later, looking just the same as when he'd gone in, except perhaps a bit sterner. Without a word, he walked past the still-shaking Woolsey and took Faro's reins from Hobie.

Garner mounted up, then just sat there for a minute, lips pursed, staring at the house.

"Find what you were lookin' for?" Sheriff Watson asked around his pipe stem.

"Wasn't looking for anything in particular," Garner replied. He reached into his vest pocket, and pulled out his fixings pouch. For not the first time, Hobie considered taking up smoking. It seemed like the thing to do when a fellow was too choked up to do much else.

"Sufferin' Jesus," Garner said bitterly, and gave his cigarette a lick. "Somebody should've drowned Donny Belasco when he was a pup."

"Better'n that," Sheriff Watson said thickly, frowning. "Somebody should'a shot his pa before he met his ma. Goddamned little sonofabitch."

Garner lit his smoke. "I reckon that's an insult to female dogs everywhere, Sheriff," he said, and shook out the match. "Which way'd they take off?"

"To the west, as far as we could tell," Sheriff Watson said, pointing with his pipe stem. "We followed as best we could till the signs petered out in the foothills." When Garner looked at him, he shrugged and added, "There ain't a decent tracker anywhere around these parts."

Garner nodded. "Well, we've got a couple of fair trackers. We'll do the best we can."

Despite everything, Hobie felt a small surge of pride at Garner's description of himself as a "fair tracker." From Garner, it was high praise, especially since Garner had put Hobie in the same class as himself. Hobie stood up a little straighter.

Deputy Trevor was helping Woolsey to his horse by that time. The reporter still looked a little weak—not to mention a tad green around the gills—but he was making progress.

Hobie, for the moment feeling a little important, ventured, "You can still turn back, Mr. Woolsey. I mean, if it's too upsettin' for you."

All he got back from Woolsey was a quick, pained glare.

"Just tryin' to be nice," Hobie muttered under his breath, and turned his attention back to Garner and Sheriff Watson.

". . . up that pass?" Garner was saying, arm outstretched, finger pointing.

"Yeah," the sheriff replied, then scowled and relit his pipe. "One thing," he said, puffing. He blew out the match. "Annie had her a little silver heart locket that she always wore. Bess Singleton, the woman that helped us fix her up for burying, said she weren't wearin' it, and the fellers couldn't find it in the house. If you find these bastards, and they've got it, we'd kinda like to have it back. Bess recollected Annie tellin' her that it was a keepsake, been in the family for years. She wants to send it to Annie's sister, back in Iowa."

Garner nodded. "I'll see what I can do."

Saddle leather creaked as Trevor boosted Woolsey up on his rental horse, and he slouched there, glasses fogged, both hands white-knuckled around the saddle horn, hair hanging in his face.

"Mr. Woolsey?" Hobie asked quietly. "You all right?"

Woolsey hissed, "Fine," through clenched teeth, without so much as a glance in Hobie's direction.

"Reckon he ain't got much stomach for it," Trevor said as he swung up on his gray. "Reckon I don't either. The burnin's are easier to take. At least the fire eats up all the . . ." He stopped, and made a face. "The fire cleans it all up, I guess."

Woolsey groaned.

"King?" said Trevor, gathering his reins. "You see anything to help us out?"

"Nope," Garner replied. "Just that Donny hasn't changed a whit." He backed Faro clear of the group of horses, tipped his hat, and said, "Thank you kindly, Sheriff. Hobie?"

"Yessir," Hobie said eagerly, hopped up on Fly, and gave Charlie Blue's lead rope a couple of turns around his saddle horn. "Ready."

Garner rode on out, Hobie and the mule following.

Dear God, Woolsey was thinking as he jogged west, behind the others. Dear God in Heaven.

He'd wanted a good story, a great story. He'd wanted it as grisly and gruesome and ghastly as possible. But what he'd seen in there . . .

He reined in the black just in time to lean over and throw up again, spattering his boot in the process. A quick glance to the front told him that no one had seen. Right at the moment, he wasn't sure whether he wanted them to or not. It would have been nice to have one of them come back, clasp him on the shoulder, and say,

"There, there, Woolsey, old man. There, there. Happens to the best of us."

But no one did, and so he kicked at the black again and urged her into a walk. Stupid horse. No, he was stupid to have come along in the first place. Why couldn't he have just been satisfied with cooling his heels back in the comfort of Tucson, writing the story up when it came in over the telegraph?

He could have dressed it up. Made it more flamboyant.

But no, he'd just had to see for himself.

Well, he'd seen for himself, hadn't he? He'd listened to Trevor—long-haired, theatrical, "Look at me!" Trevor—begin to expound on just what Donny Belasco had done to Mrs. Cartwell and when, and that was it. He'd burst from the house and involuntarily emptied the entire contents of his stomach all over Annie Cartwell's flower garden.

Well, except for this last bit he'd just gotten rid of.

He had half a mind to just turn around and go back to Tucson.

But he looked ahead, at Trevor and Garner, he looked at Hobie—younger than he by a few years, at least, and seemingly not intimidated—and forged ahead.

"I am a certifiable idiot," he muttered.

8

A frustrated "Damn and blast it!" echoed through the rocks, and a disgusted Garner pulled Faro to a halt again. He twisted in his saddle to see what was wrong with Woolsey this time.

The others had stopped, too. Trevor was riding back toward Woolsey, who brought up the rear—as usual—and who had dismounted and was jumping up and down on his hat.

"Sure got a knot in his drawers this time," Hobie remarked as he and Garner jogged back toward Woolsey.

"Acts like a damn three-year-old kid," Garner replied.

"It's broken, I tell you!" Woolsey was insisting to Trevor. "This damned horse is broken! Defective! I'll take that livery to court when I get back!" He went to jump on his hat again and missed.

"Best pick that up and treat it kinder," said Garner as evenly as he could, which wasn't any too even. "It's the only one you got. There aren't any haberdashers down this way."

Woolsey looked up with a jerk. "Oh, shut up," he spat.

Garner ground his teeth. "Look, you sorry little peckerwood . . ."

Trevor, who had dismounted, picked up Woolsey's mare's left foreleg and studied the underside of the hoof for a second. He looked up at Garner. "Stone bruise is all," he said, and let the hoof down.

"You been checkin' that horse's feet?" Garner asked Woolsey, and this time he made no attempt to cover his anger. "You been picking them out every morning?"

Woolsey's features bunched up. "What?"

"He don't have the least notion, King," said Trevor with a shrug.

Garner glared at Woolsey in pure, unadulterated disgust. "That does it. We're leaving you here. You've been a pain in the butt since we started out. First it was jabber, jabber, jabber about all kinds of crud that nobody gave a hoot about. Then you wouldn't open your mouth for honey till we stopped to camp. Then it was bitchin' about the food, bitchin' about your bed, bitchin' about everything. The only time you kept your pie hole closed was when Marcus, here, was spoutin' off about all sorts of stuff he doesn't know jackshit about."

"Hey!" shouted Trevor.

"You keep sayin'," Garner continued, "as how you want to write this story so bad, but you puke at the first sight of it!"

"That was unadulterated gore back there!" cried Woolsey, and not happily.

"That's what it's all about, you jackass," snarled Garner, and started to rein Faro about.

He stopped, though, when Woolsey spat, "You can't leave me out here alone!" It came out with all the assuredness of the well-educated, and then, rather suddenly, his face was lined with what Garner knew was latent terror. "F-freedom of the press!" he added lamely.

"You're free to walk on out of here, boy," Garner said smugly, enjoying Woolsey's discomfort. "You can make it back to the Cartwell place, shank's mare, in less than a day. There's water there. Then another half day to Baker. Don't push your luck."

Hobie leaned across the space between his horse and Garner's. "Boss?" he whispered. "I don't like him much myself, but he won't last an hour out here on his lonesome."

"Not my problem," Garner barked so harshly that Hobie nearly jumped out of his saddle. Garner tempered his tone a bit. "Oh, hell. Have him write his goddamn way back to town. And if I remember right, aren't you the one who was givin' that bleeding-heart speech back in the hotel lobby?"

Hobie had the great good sense to look a little pained.

Trevor pushed aside his sand-colored mop to scratch the back of his neck. "Now, King, he may not be your problem, but he's mine, and we ain't leavin' him. Hobie, get the supplies off that mule'a yours and spread 'em out betwixt us."

"Mule?" Woolsey gulped, and eyed Charlie Blue. "You don't intend that I should ride that—"

"No," Garner interrupted. "He'll slow us down even more than he has been."

"Can't be helped, King."

"The hell it can't," Garner snapped. "Hobie, give me over my share of coffee, ham, and jerky. Some beans and a water bag, too. And grain for Faro."

Hobie blinked. "Boss, you're not—"

But Garner ignored him. "Marcus," he said, "I quit."

Trevor worked his jaw, then hiked his nose in the air. "You can't quit. You're signed on for the duration."

"Says who?"

"Says me," Trevor said angrily. He jabbed a thumb toward his chest. "I'm the one what gave you that badge Hobie's wearin'. I'm in charge."

Garner snatched up the water bag that Hobie offered and hung it from his saddle horn. Its weight thumped moistly against his leg.

"Yeah," he said. "That's another thing. Hobie, keep the badge if you want. And you can stay or go. I don't much care."

"Let him leave, Deputy," said Woolsey, the bone of contention personified. He crossed his bony arms. "Let them both desert us. We'll be just fine without some old has-been and a schoolboy."

"What do you mean, schoolboy?" Hobie asked, full of umbrage.

Garner was sorely tempted to just get down off his horse and punch Woolsey square in the jaw, but then Hobie seemed to have another thought. He said, "Boss? How they gonna track anything without us?" and Garner turned his anger on the boy.

"Shut up, Hobie!"

"You just keep your backside planted where it is, Hobie," Trevor ordered, his voice as loud and angry as Garner's. "We need you to trail these birds, now that the great King Garner has showed himself a quitter."

"You're not out here to track those boys, Marcus," Garner growled, dropping his voice. "You're out here leadin' a goddamn circus. Well, I say good luck to you and your big top and your pet clown." He flicked his eyes toward Woolsey. "You're gonna need it."

And with that, he gave the food sack a couple of turns around his saddle horn, reined Faro about, and took off, up into the hills.

"Good riddance to bad rubbish!" said Woolsey, his nose in the air. "I never liked him anyway. The man has shown his true colors, I tell you. Taking off and going home! Of all the—"

"Shut the hell up, Woolsey," Trevor snapped. "Just close your damn pie hole."

While the two of them bickered, Hobie watched Garner disappear into the distant rocks. If Trevor and Woolsey were oblivious, Hobie knew exactly what Garner was doing. He was cutting north of Belasco and Martindale's feeble, weathered trail, not following it at all. Hobie figured Garner would keep on until he found a stretch of ground that wouldn't hold track, and then he'd cut back down, miles ahead. He was trying to lose the rest of them.

Smart, thought Hobie, a bit too self-satisfied. But not smart enough.

If Garner figured Hobie was too dense to just keep right on track, too stupid to hold his nose to it, he had another think coming. Sure, Trevor might lose the trail. He was probably a pretty fair deputy, but he wasn't too much at tracking. Hobie'd seen enough to know that.

Well, he'd show Garner.

He finished unpacking Charlie Blue, divvied up the remaining goods, then put the injured black's saddle on the mule. It didn't exactly fit—the tree was too narrow for the broad Charlie Blue—but he did the best he could with it, more for the mule's comfort than Woolsey's.

Then he aimed the black mare back toward the Cartwell place and smacked her on the rump. At least she'd find water there.

Woolsey, who'd been busy bickering with Deputy Trevor, wheeled about. "What are you doing?" he asked, his voice suddenly tinged with hysteria.

"I'm settin' your horse loose," Hobie said, as if talking to a two-year-old. Any respect he'd had for Woolsey was long gone. Schoolboy, his Aunt Fanny!

"Why?" Woolsey cried. "Why did you do that, you idiot?"

Hobie just started at him, amazed that any human person could be so stupid.

Trevor swung up on his gray. "Get on the damn mule," he growled, and Hobie could tell that Garner's departure had hit Trevor a lot harder than he was admitting.

"Only if someone will ride back and retrieve my horse," Woolsey insisted, and stubbornly stood his ground. "I'm responsible for that worthless creature."

"Get on the mule," Trevor repeated through clenched teeth.

"No."

Then Trevor pulled his gun, and Hobie gulped. So did Woolsey.

"You get on that mule," Trevor growled, "or so help me, God, I'll shoot you in the foot."

Woolsey, who had grown considerably paler in the span of two seconds, clambered aboard the sizable Charlie Blue, who immediately pinned his long ears back.

Trying not to smile, Hobie said, "I'd be careful if I was you, Mr. Woolsey. That mule doesn't appear to have been rode in a spell."

"If ever," Trevor muttered, holstering his pistol. He gathered his reins. "Which way, Hobie?"

"Just like we been goin', I reckon."

Trevor pursed his lips. "You don't think we oughta follow King?"

Charlie Blue gave a half-hearted buck and Woolsey went halfway off, then clumsily hauled himself back up and clung desperately to the mule's roached mane.

Hobie and Trevor pretended not to see.

Hobie shook his head. "Reckon Woolsey is right. He's deserted us. Headin' for home," he lied. "He was pretty mad." That part was sure the truth, though.

"That he was, that he was," Trevor said, looking up toward the place where Garner had disappeared into the hills. He sighed. "Well, it's up to you, now, Hobie. Not that I want to make you nervous or nothing," he added with a grin that wasn't quite convincing.

"Yes, sir," said Hobie with a nod. "I'll do my best." He looked back at Woolsey, who had both hands knotted into Charlie Blue's short mane. Charlie Blue looked every bit as annoyed with the situation as Woolsey did, but a lot more confident.

Hobie said, "Deputy, you figure we oughta tie him on?"

Garner had cut south again, and was working his way down toward Belasco and Martindale's track. Or at least, he hoped he was.

He knew these hills, and he also knew that there was really only one decent trail through them without detouring four miles north or ten miles south. And he didn't think Martindale was smart enough—or Donny Belasco was patient enough—to travel either of those.

He'd ridden north, making the best time he could. It

was a sight better than he'd been making, leading that crew of jokers. Then he'd gone on west, galloping when he could, walking when he had to, and had gone nearly all the way through this range of hills before he began to slowly drift south.

But the sun was moving low in the sky, and Faro was tired.

So was he, come to think of it. He found a likely-looking place with some rock shelter, dismounted, and hobbled Faro.

He unsaddled Faro, fed and watered him, and to the sound of molars contentedly grinding grain, began to curry the horse. He did some of his best thinking when he had his hands on a horse.

So far, he'd been concentrating on just following Belasco and Martindale, but now it struck him that he'd be better off thinking about their destination rather than their path. Now, where would Belasco and Martindale head next?

Donny's taste wasn't for farm wives, that was for sure, and he'd probably killed the two that he had out of sheer desperation. Which meant that since busting out of Yuma, the lust for it was on him harder than ever.

Thank God there weren't any homesteads out this way. At least, none that Garner knew of. Too dry, too desolate to ranch or farm, either one. The nearest water—and possible female company—was a couple of days' ride to the southwest, in a dinky little town called High Draw, about twenty miles north of the border.

And that, Garner decided at last, was where Belasco and Martindale would most probably head.

What he couldn't figure out was what Martindale had been doing all these years. A man could hold off his natural proclivities for a while, sure, but for almost six years? Maybe he'd been out of the country. Maybe he'd been in jail.

Hell, maybe he'd been hog-tied in somebody's cellar or something.

It didn't much matter. What did was that Martindale and Belasco were going to be dead if it was the last thing Garner did. He wouldn't make the mistake of hauling in a sick little dog turd like Belasco again. Not unless it was over a saddle and extremely deceased.

Garner switched to the body brush, and began flicking away the grime he'd brought up with the curry. The horse swung his head back and gave Garner a little nudge with his nose and a soft nicker.

"Yeah," Garner said, momentarily relaxing into a smile. "Feels good, doesn't it, buddy?"

Up by the fire, Hobie was busy slapping together their supper and Woolsey was preoccupied with his notepad, copying something from it to a larger sheet of paper, a great many of which he'd brought along and upon which he only wrote at night.

And Marcus Trevor was occupied with taking care of the horses. Woolsey's mule, to be more precise.

Trevor had mixed feelings about how the day had gone. Things started out just fine in town with Sheriff Watson. Trevor had made some quotable quotes— which he'd spied Woolsey taking down on his notepad—but the day had started to go downhill the second they'd set foot in the Cartwell house. He hadn't had the slightest idea that Woolsey would react the way he did.

Trevor had thought reporters were tough.

Apparently, he'd been wrong.

"Ouch!" he yelped, and smacked the mule in the head.

"What?" called Hobie, half rising out of his squat near the fire.

"Nothin'," Trevor replied, and the smarting hand he was shaking became the hand he waved at Hobie. That damn mule had a hard head, by God! "Blasted mule bit me."

Charlie Blue made a second attempt to snag his sleeve, as if to prove the point.

Woolsey turned his head toward them for a moment and smirked. "You see?" he said before he dipped his pen and bent his head to his work again.

You'd better be writing some awful nice things about me, you dumb slicker, Trevor thought. He gave his hand a final shake, then waved a warning fist at Charlie Blue. He commenced brushing and currying again.

Garner gone. That just about beat everything, didn't it? He surely hadn't counted on it, hadn't even seen it coming. Garner was, by reputation, one of the most pig-headed men west of the Mississippi. Once Trevor had signed him on, he'd figured to just about have him for life.

A bad day, yessir.

But he still had Hobie. The kid was a pretty fair tracker. He wondered if Garner had trained him, then decided no, he probably hadn't. Not much call for tracking and trailing when all you had to do was sit on your stoop sipping bourbon whiskey by the case. No, Hobie just had talent. Something that Trevor himself had never possessed, at least for tracking.

But he had flair. By damn, he could put on a show with the best of them. He'd learned early in his career that other men might do the actual work, but most of them had no stomach for reporters and questions and celebrity. Most of them just did their jobs, then crawled back into their holes and didn't come back out until there was a job to be done.

Not Trevor. He could do the least and get the most out of it of any man in the U.S. Marshals Service. He was genuinely proud of this, although he had never admitted it to anyone save Annie. And he'd only told Annie because, well, he had to tell somebody.

Because along with the pride—getting good publicity for the U.S. Marshals Service was important and necessary, wasn't it?—came a small degree of shame. He wasn't the best tracker, wasn't the best shot, wasn't the best at picking up—or following up—clues, and he knew it. No, he always managed to rope somebody into going along with him for that, whatever the situation called for. Somebody unassuming, somebody who avoided notoriety, somebody who'd fade back into the woodwork the moment the job was done.

Somebody like Garner.

Sometimes, Trevor felt that his growing reputation wasn't exactly warranted, that he didn't deserve all this acclaim. But when, during one of his weaker moments, he'd confided this to Annie, she'd said, "Baby, don't you fret over it anymore. You pick the fellers to go with you, don't you? You're in charge of the whole operation, aren't you? And if you don't get your man, nobody takes the blame but you, poor lamb. Marc, darlin', I don't see why you shouldn't get all the glory." And then she'd kissed him, and he'd felt a whole lot better.

Still, every once in a while, he had a pang of guilt.

They were getting fewer and farther between, though.

He put down the brushes, smacked Charlie Blue on

the rump, squared his shoulders, and walked toward the fire. Bad day or no, he'd make the best of it. He always did.

"Is it dinner yet, Hobie?" he asked, and smiled wide.

Their campsite was sheltered on two sides by rocks, with a sheer drop-off on the third, and a clear view of anything that might pass—or approach—on the fourth. Martindale congratulated himself on choosing well, but didn't dwell on it. He was busy thinking bitter thoughts about Belasco.

Belasco had built them a little fire, and was presently scooping Arbuckle's into a tin coffeepot.

"We're 'bout outta water," Martindale commented sullenly. He hadn't liked the way Belasco was looking at him lately. He couldn't put his finger on it, but it was just . . . funny.

Made his skin crawl.

Made him mad.

"Yes indeed," said Belasco, all chipper, like he was having a vacation. Humming, he poured water into the coffeepot. Martindale had never met anybody so god-damn agreeable as Donny Belasco was. It gave him the collywobbles.

Belasco continued, "Don't you fret about it. We'll be riding into High Draw tomorrow, old chum. They'll have all the water anyone could possibly want."

The thought of a town brightened Martindale a bit. "Maybe I can get me a beer," he said.

"Yes indeed, you certainly can," Belasco responded cheerily, and set the pot on the fire. "Get two beers, get three, get a whole barrel!"

Then another thought occurred, and Martindale scowled. "You gonna cut you a whore?"

"Ah, you're too clever for me, Vince," said Belasco, pursing his lips. He pulled the food bag over and proceeded to pull out a hunk of smoke-cured venison, courtesy of the Cartwells' larder. "Can't put anything over on you, my comrade, old pal, partner. No, sirree, Bob."

"Stop makin' fun of me," Martindale growled. His hand slid around to the grip of his six-gun.

"Heaven forfend!" Belasco said, theatrically slapping a hand to his chest. "The last thing I'd do is make fun of you. Why, we're partners, aren't we? *Amigos* to the end!"

Martindale slowly relaxed his gun hand, but didn't move it. "I reckon," he said slowly. "But you're gonna bring the law down on us if you keep on cutting them girls like you been. You gotta, you know, kinda space it out."

Belasco seemed untroubled. He sliced off a thick hunk of the meat and tossed it to Martindale. Without thinking, the hand that had rested on the butt of his gun flew up to catch the meat.

Belasco smiled at him. The sonofabitch.

If he didn't stop cutting those gals every fifteen minutes, he was gonna get Martindale hanged right along with him.

Now, burning, that was different. You could make that look like it was an accident. He'd burnt up three men just before they'd put him in prison, hadn't he? Made it look like a brushfire had taken their cabin, whoosh! And, oh, how they'd hollered. It made him real satisfied, even after all this time, just thinking about it.

In fact, when that posse had arrested him, he'd thought that was what they were taking him in for, the burning. Except that one of them called him the wrong name, and said, This'll teach you to steal from Clyde

Roth, Winchell! before somebody else had cracked him over the skull with a rifle butt.

Then later, while he was in jail, he saw a poster for himself. Course, it was without the beard, and it described him as two inches shorter than he stood. But it was for him, all right. It had said, "Wanted, Dead or Alive."

And for once, Martindale had done the smart thing and kept his mouth shut.

The funny thing was, about a year ago through the prison grapevine, he'd heard that he'd been hanged over in Texas or New Mexico or somewhere. Why, he had to feel himself to make certain he was still there!

It was too bad about Piggy, he thought, gnawing on his meat. Pignose and he would have had some fine times, because Piggy liked to burn things up, too. Not like this snot-nosed shit, all fussy and prissy and shaving every damn morning, cutting up his meat and trimming his mustache and cleaning his fingernails. His clothes were always clean too, except when he'd been at some woman with that shiny razor of his.

A waste of good water, Martindale thought, slowly shaking his shaggy head. All that good water, just dumped on a bunch of bloody clothes.

"A comment, Friend Vincent?" Belasco said. His eyes glittered brightly across the fire.

"Huh?" Martindale responded.

"Ah," said Belasco sagely. "Just as I thought. Should I make biscuits?"

"Hell, no," said Martindale, and made a face.

"Ah, well," Belasco said with a shrug, and neatly cut off another bite of meat. He smiled. "To each his own."

9

The next afternoon, Belasco and Martindale rode into the sleepy little town of High Draw, scattering fluttering chickens before them. A crude sign on the outskirts had proclaimed, "POP. 67 & GROWING," but Martindale thought it must be an exaggeration. Appeared more like twenty-seven to him.

"Don't look like much," Martindale said as they tethered their horses to the rail out in front of the Joker's Wild Saloon.

"Looks can be deceiving," replied Belasco.

They stepped up onto the sidewalk and through the batwing doors of the bar. Martindale's eyes barely had a chance to grow accustomed to the dim light when Belasco said, "Why don't you take our horses down to the livery, Vincent? I may be here some time."

Sullenly, Martindale said, "I want a beer. Why do I got to do everything?"

But Belasco replied, "Why, I'll order one for you,

chum," and he said it so happily that Martindale was outside, leading the horses down the street—and kicking a couple of scrawny chickens aside—before he knew what was happening.

There was indeed a beer waiting for him when he hiked back up the street and went into the saloon. The beer was warm and flat, but he was glad to get it, and downed it in the time it took Belasco to set his eyes on a likely-looking whore.

She was young, maybe sixteen or seventeen, Martindale thought, and plug-ugly. Not like Belasco usually liked them, but then, beggars couldn't be choosers and she was the only girl in the bar. Martindale smiled and ordered himself another beer. She looked real happy to have a customer.

Boy, was she going to be in for a surprise.

Belasco brought her over to the table.

"Vince, I'd like you to meet Pansy," he said.

"Hey, Pansy," Martindale muttered dully, and took a drink of his second beer.

She slid into a chair. "Hey, back," she said. She looked up at Belasco and batted her eyes. "Can I have one'a them, mister?"

"A beer?" Belasco said. "Why, certainly!" He waved at the bartender and gestured before he slid into the chair next to her.

He picked up her hand, stroking it like it was made of porcelain. "Pansy was just telling me that she's from the great state of California, Vincent. Isn't that interesting?"

Pansy looked at Belasco like he was the Second Coming.

"Sure," said Martindale. He looked around for a menu. "This place got food?"

Pansy was staring into Belasco's eyes.

"Darling?" Belasco prompted softly. "Does this establishment serve any meals?"

She smiled. Still staring limply at Belasco, she said, "Joe can make free sandwiches if'n you ask. We got some beef, I think." She let out a little sigh.

Martindale scraped back his chair and stood up. "You want one?" he asked.

Without taking his eyes from Pansy's, Belasco said, "Thank you. If you wouldn't mind."

Martindale went over to the bar and ordered two sandwiches, both with plenty of peppers and ketchup. He supposed that if they weren't big enough, he could always get himself another. In his experience, bars didn't make good sandwiches—or big ones—unless you paid for them. Mostly stale or moldy bread, and you had to hunt for the meat.

While he waited, he leaned back against the bar and studied Belasco. Making a damn fool of himself, that's what he was doing. How anybody could coo over a gal like Pansy, even if he was only gonna gut her later on, was beyond Martindale. Why, her eyes were pretty near crossed! She had lank, brown hair and crooked teeth, and a nose that had been broken a few times. A genuine dog. She'd likely start barking or panting any minute, if you asked Martindale.

But then, nobody had.

Martindale carried the sandwiches back to the table. They were as he had expected: brown bread a few days old, and where it wasn't hard enough to break a pitchfork, the bread was beginning to mold. When he peeked inside at the meat, what there was of it was curling up and smelled funny, kind of sweet and nasty.

Well, what the hell, he thought, and smeared the

ketchup to cover it. He bit in. It didn't taste too awful bad. It beat the hell out of Belasco's cooking, that was for sure.

Belasco hadn't touched his. He was busy talking sweet to Pansy. Now, Belasco hadn't been inside with that farmer's wife for more than five minutes before she'd started squealing like a stuck pig. Martindale supposed Belasco had missed this part, the part where he played nice as pie, got them all goggle-eyed and fluttery.

This, miraculously, he understood.

He understood how men in general—and Belasco in particular—could have pet times. He had a pet time of his own. The part he liked best was when they screamed, the first panicked notes of it. That real high, helpless sound men made when they were going to die and knew it, when the fire was first licking at their skin and sizzling their eyeballs.

Once he'd burnt a fellow that had passed out before he threw him in. What a waste! Not a sound, not a goddamn peep!

And so he sat there and ate his sandwich, then Belasco's, and drank a total of three beers while Belasco billed and cooed with the little bitch, who was getting sillier by the moment.

And he watched Belasco. Watched him run the tip of his finger around the girl's ears, one by one. Watched him gently graze her throat with his palm while she giggled.

And he thought, If only you knowed what he has in that pocket of his, girlie-girl.

Something shiny. Something sharp.

He smiled, but somewhat grimly. His stomach felt sort of funny, probably from the bad sandwiches, and he was beginning to get a little annoyed at Belasco. After all, why did he get to have all the fun? Here they were, the only customers in this rat-bag saloon that probably was crowded when there were half-a-dozen drinkers in it, and Belasco could take that girl upstairs and gag her and have himself a real good time with nobody the wiser. Until the next morning, that is, when somebody went up and found her.

But him? He couldn't have any fun in town, because what he liked to do was showy, by God. Why, everybody came to a fire!

He smirked proudly, and ordered himself another drink. Whiskey, this time.

He took it down in one gulp, then ordered another. It wasn't fair, he thought. Not fair at all. Outside, it was already dark, and Belasco was going to have his fun real soon. But Martindale? Poor old Martindale would just be down at the livery, waiting along with the horses, sitting around and scratching his ass.

He drank his second whiskey, and his stomach lurched to the side. He stood up.

"Leaving?" asked Belasco. It was the first time he'd looked anywhere but at the girl's face in the last half hour.

Suddenly, that lurching Martindale had felt got to feeling a whole lot worse and a whole lot lower.

"Be down at the livery," he said, moving quickly toward the door, afraid he'd shit his pants in front of God and everybody.

He just made it to the alley in time, and squatted down behind a barrel.

Donny Belasco watched Martindale's hasty exit into the night, then turned back toward the fair Pansy.

Well, not so fair, but a fellow couldn't have everything.

"Tell me, my love," he said, tracing her palm with his fingertip. "Does this lovely metropolis have a sheriff's office?" It was better to be safe than sorry, although he'd gone so far now that he doubted he could stop.

Fortunately, she batted her lashes and said, "Mister, we ain't got but sixty-seven souls in High Draw, and most of 'em live outside town. Only way we could afford a sheriff is if he paid us!"

She seemed to think this highly amusing, and broke out into a braying horse laugh. Her breath moved over him in an acrid cloud, and for a moment he thought she might be better matched to Martindale than to him.

But he stood up and held out his hand.

"Shall we go upstairs, my pet?" he asked, all charm. "I have something very bright and shiny to show you. Something glittery."

"Glittery?" she said, head cocked. She rose, too, and melted against him. "I thought you was never gonna ask me, mister," she said, and led him up the stairs.

Three squats later, Martindale figured himself to be about empty. He was angry, though. He would have liked to get that goddamned bartender down here at the livery, he thought, just to show him what happened to fellows who gave bad meat to their customers.

The bastard never would have served a bad sandwich again, that was for sure, not after Martindale got through with him.

He leaned forward—he was outside the barn, sitting near the manure pile—and wobbled to his feet. It wasn't fair that he always had the runs when he got sick. He remembered his brothers always puked, plain and simple, but him? He always had to shit like a god-damn geyser. He took a few steps. His belly felt all right again, at least for the moment.

He wandered up to the front. The sign said "Martin's Livery," but it sure wasn't much. Just a wooden struc-ture, big enough for maybe four horses and a rental buggy, with one corral out at the side. Besides his nag and Belasco's, the only animals in the place were a cou-ple of roosting hens.

Inside, by the light of a lantern, the old geezer who owned the place was playing checkers across a blan-keted hay bale with another fellow, and when Martin-dale stumbled up to the door, he raised his hand in recognition.

"Howdy again," the old geezer said, and held up a bottle. "Care for a belt?"

It was fully dark by then, and Belasco had likely started in on the girl. He would have gagged her, of course, would have had to, to keep her quiet. But he still got to have his fun while Martindale waited.

Not fair.

Martindale said, "Howdy," right back, and sat down. "Don't mind if I do."

He took a belt, then wiped at his mouth, and passed the bottle on. "This barn ain't got no winders," he said, looking around.

"Nope," said the old stableman, studying the checkerboard. "I do believe you've set yourself up, there, Harry."

Harry scratched at his ear.

Martindale said, "No back door, either?"

"You want back doors, take your business over to Connerville," the stableman said without looking at him. He jumped three of his opponent's checkers, landed on the far side, then smugly said, "King me, Harry."

"Aw, horse hockey," muttered Harry.

"You don't have to get snippy," Martindale said, standing. "I was just askin'."

"You goin' someplace?" the hostler asked.

"Just gonna tack up my mounts," Martindale said. "My partner and me figure to ride out tonight."

"Well, you're paid till morning," the man said, shrugging. "No skin off my nose." He turned his attention back to the game.

Martindale leisurely saddled his horse, then Belasco's, then slipped an unlit lantern off the far wall and its handle over his arm. He led the horses from the barn and tethered them at the far end of the corral, then took a slow walk around the entire structure, sloshing just enough kerosene here and there, around the outside, so that it would burn nice and even. He stopped when he was down to a half inch of fuel. Carefully replacing the lantern's top, he pulled out a sulphur tip and lit the wick.

He walked up to the door, swinging the lantern in his hand.

The stableman looked up, and he must had seen something in Martindale's face, because his brow furrowed. "Where'd you get that lamp?" he asked.

"Next time, I'll try Connerville," Martindale said, and tossed the lantern.

There was just enough kerosene left that when it shattered about the wall, it also doused a bale of straw. Both burst into flames.

Harry and the old stable owner shot up immediately, grabbed horse blankets, and began to beat at the flames.

The two chickens in the barn were smarter. They

made a beeline for the door and scooted out between Martindale's boots.

Martindale backed out, ripped the leather lift-latch off the inside before he swung the door closed, and settled the crossbar into place.

Then he walked quickly around the building's perimeter, lighting matches as he went, touching them to the walls, which immediately whooshed up into flame.

"Mighty dry here, gents," he whispered, smiling. "Yessir, mighty dry. Whole place is nothin' but kindlin'."

By the time he got back to the horses, the men had begun to scream.

The whole town was up in arms by this time. People streamed down the road, armed with buckets and blankets and shovels. Even the bartender from the Joker's Wild rushed past him.

"What happened? What happened?" cried a little man halfway into a tattered buckskin jacket.

Martindale shook his head. "She just went up," he said with a shrug. "Told 'em not to set that lantern so near the bales."

He was having a wonderful time.

Inside, beneath the groans of timber and the crackle and roar of fire swiftly consuming the structure, the pleas for help had changed to wordless cries of pain and fear.

He loved this part.

He untied the two horses and slowly led them through the panicky crowd and up to the vacated saloon, keeping his face down. He knew he was smirking. Couldn't help it.

Oh, there was nothing like a fire!

Belasco, disheveled, his shirt blotched with blood, came busting out the doors at just about the time he reached the saloon.

"Reckon you had you a good time, too," Martindale said, looking him up and down.

Belasco turned his head as a man shrieked inside the livery. Martindale didn't know which one. Maybe the old stable owner.

"You fool!" Belasco snarled, and grabbed his reins. "You idiot!"

"What?" Martindale asked innocently. Belasco was already mounting. "Hell, I just wanted to have a little fun, too, y'know! I mean, you got to—"

"Shut up!" snapped Donny.

Down the street, buckets were being swiftly passed, but it was no use. The men had stopped crying out. Maybe they were dead, Martindale thought, or maybe they were just beyond hollering. The only sounds now were those of the fire and the crowd, and the fire was spreading. A second line had formed from the water trough to the neighboring building. It was a gunsmith's shop, if he remembered rightly.

"Say!" he said suddenly, and broke out in a wide grin. "You reckon they got any loose gunpowder at that smith's shop? You know, like could mayhap blow it sky high?"

"Get on your goddamn horse," Belasco said through gritted teeth.

"Couldn't we just wait till—"

"Now," Belasco hissed.

Martindale sighed. There Belasco went again, ruining all his fun.

Reluctantly, he swung up on his horse, gathered his reins, and followed Belasco out of town, into the night, at a slow jog.

Behind them, the fire was swiftly spreading. High Draw was going up in flames.

10

Late the next afternoon when Garner rode over the hills that surrounded High Draw, he saw the haze of smoke before he made out the town. He didn't need anybody to tell him that Martindale had been here. More than half the town had been burnt to the ground, and some of it was still feebly smoking.

Bandannas tied over their blackened faces, exhausted men and a few red-eyed women toiled their way through the ashen rubble of perhaps eight to ten buildings. He couldn't tell exactly how many. The workers wearily shoveled aside debris, poured out buckets of water that hissed on hot spots.

Under the bleary stares of the firefighters, Garner rode slowly up the street—cluttered with burnt timbers, broken glass, and an uncommon number of soot-dusted, addled chickens—and stopped at the Joker's Wild Saloon. The fire must have started at what had once been the livery, and spread through the buildings on the far side of it. The saloon and three other structures were all that was left of High Draw.

"Sonofabitch," Garner muttered grimly, and tethered Faro to the rail within easy reach of the water trough. The horse drank greedily.

There was only one man in the bar. He was as grime-caked as the ones outside, and he was sprawled, half-asleep, on one of the three scarred tables, arm over his face.

"Awake?" Garner asked from the doorway.

"Reckon," the man answered wearily, and rubbed at his eyes.

Garner walked on in. "When'd it happen?" There was no need to qualify the question.

"Last night," the haggard man replied, and sat up. His shirt was scorched, and one cuff of his pants was burnt away. He got off the table as if he were sore all over, slowly made his way behind the planks that served as a bar, and said, "What'll you have?"

"Beer," Garner replied, and plunked down a coin. He looked out the window, toward the ruined buildings. "You had any strangers through lately?" he asked, although he already knew the answer.

"One of 'em's a dark man," he continued. "Middle-sized, thick-built, brow like a porch overhang, looks part-Mexican. Scarred face, but he usually wears a beard to cover it. Likes to start fires."

"The bastard," the bartender said grimly, and slid Garner his beer. "Why, I talked to him! Lots of folks did. He was right down there when they sounded the cry, right down there by the livery, lookin' all innocent-like when he'd locked up Harry and old Jess in there to die, done it a'purpose. We should'a strung him up on sight, that's what we should'a done!"

"Wish you had," Garner replied in all honesty, and took a long, satisfying gulp of his beer. It was his first drink since leaving home, and he figured he deserved it.

"I'm real grieved to hear about your losses," he added truthfully with a sad shake of his head. "Was there another fellow with him? Younger, good-lookin', reddish hair, keeps himself up nice. The kind of boy old ladies are crazy about."

Beneath the grime, the barkeep's face grew darker. "There sure was. That godless little bastard 'bout near killed poor Pansy."

Garner paused, the beer mug at his lips. "*Near* killed her?"

"Tied her up, gagged her, and sliced her damn ear clean off!" the bartender said. "How'm I supposed to make any cash money off a whore with one ear? Answer me that!"

Garner set down his beer hard enough that it splashed out over his hand. "Where is she?" he said, wiping his fingers on his shirt.

"Upstairs. And who the hell are you, anyway?"

"Garner," he said, turning toward the stairs. "King Garner." He took the steps two at a time.

Pansy's head was wrapped tight with bandages all the way around. Not so much as a hair stuck out anywhere, although a large, dried rusty stain showed where Belasco had begun to work on her. Her eyes were lined with red and her face was pale.

"He showed it to me," she sniffed weakly. "Just held it up and showed it to me. And he took it with him!" She began to cry again, and rested her fingers alongside her head. "Oh, it hurts, it hurts!"

Garner ground his teeth. She'd been carrying on for some time, and it was beginning to grate on him.

"Ma'am?" he said again, trying to get her attention. "Miss?" When she cried harder, he said, "Goddamn it, Pansy!"

This jolted her a bit, and she stared at him wide-eyed, no longer crying, but hiccupping softly.

"Did he say where they were going?" When this produced nothing but a blank stare, he tried again more gently. "Him and his partner. Did they talk about it at all?"

She launched into waterworks again, but before she could get a good start, Garner took her by the shoulders and shook her hard.

She hauled off and slapped him across the face.

"What'd you do that for?" he roared.

"You was hysterical!" she shouted angrily, then hiccupped.

"*I* was hysterical?" he said, leaning back out of her range. "Listen, sweetheart, one ear or not, I'm about ready to haul off and slug you if I don't get a straight answer pretty goddamn soon."

She sniffed. "You're not very nice. Here I am, practically mutilated, and all you can do is—"

"I'm gonna count to five," a glowering Garner interrupted. "One. Two. Three . . ."

"All right, all right," she said, and paused to blow her nose on a corner of the sheets. "No, he didn't say squat, 'cept"—she paused to hiccup—"to tell me all kinds of nasty, pretty lies, and about how I had eyes all blue-green, like a sea of grass," she said, suddenly dreamy. She hiccupped again. "Like the vast Sargasso Sea, he said. I remember that rightly, 'cause I made him say it over four, maybe five times. The vast Sargasso Sea.

Ain't that pretty? You know where that grass is, mister? I'd surely like to take a look for myself."

"Pansy . . ."

"And then he went and tied me up and gagged me and sliced off my ear!" she said, suddenly furious all over again. "Just cut it right off with that razor of his! And showed it to me! What kinda feller does that, mister?" Another hiccup. "What kinda feller cuts off your ear and then just puts it in his pocket like it was a . . . a . . ."

She was obviously stumped for words, so Garner said, "The kind that would have sliced off the other one and slit your throat, too, if somebody hadn't hollered, 'Fire.'"

She wasn't really listening. "Calvin's awful mad," she muttered.

"Calvin?"

She pointed toward the floor. "Downstairs at the bar. Owns this place. It don't seem right, do it? Him bein' mad 'cause I got hurt." She hiccuped again. "Don't it seem to you he oughta be het up at the feller what done it to me?"

"He is, trust me." Garner stood up. "And he'd be more pissed if he was having to bury you today." He didn't point out that she was damned lucky her innards hadn't ended up on a pie tin.

Oddly enough, she brightened. "Reckon that's true, mister. I reckon it is. I'll have to point that out to him."

Garner took the steps downstairs a helluva lot slower than he'd taken them up. It looked like nobody in High Draw was going to be any help whatsoever. He was glad that Belasco had been startled, and relieved that Pansy was still alive—it was a first for Belasco to leave a job unfinished, he was sure of that—but Pansy was a worthless witness. And it seemed that everybody else had been too caught up with the spreading fire to catch anything real particular about Belasco and Martindale. He'd just have to keep going the way he'd been, watching for tracks and bent brush and turned-over stones and a dozen other things.

Hobie was a damn good tracker, all right, but he had nothing on Garner. He and Trevor and that idiot, Woolsey, were likely a good day behind him.

He looked around for his beer. He figured to finish his drink off quick, then light out. There was still an hour of decent tracking time before it would grow too dark.

"Where's my drink?" he asked the barkeep.

"I dumped it," said Calvin, standing stiffly behind the bar. "Your kind don't drink here." His knuckles were white, and his jaw muscles were working.

"My kind?" Garner said cautiously. "What you talking about, friend?"

"Don't call me friend. I know you. You're King Garner."

Garner sighed. "So? I told you that."

"Reckon you don't know who I am," the bartender said with just a touch of pride.

"You're Calvin the barkeep, buddy," Garner said. He hiked a thumb toward the ceiling. "Pansy told me." Suddenly, something about the way Calvin was looking at him sent the little hairs on the back of his neck standing right up. This was the wrong conversation, and the wrong fellow to be having it with.

"Right, Mr. King Garner," said Calvin. His hands were shaking almost imperceptibly. "And I'm Calvin Farley. Know me now?"

Now all the hair on Garner's arms stood up, too. "Farley," he said. It wasn't a question.

"You killed my cousins," Calvin said quietly, his face grim. "You hid behind some stupid badge cut out of a tin can and gunned 'em down. In cold blood."

"It wasn't in cold blood. There were shooting at me," Garner said as calmly as he could under the circumstances. "And I went after 'em because they killed three people—including an officer of the law—and robbed a bank." He didn't want to have to shoot this man, didn't want to draw his gun, especially over the damn Farley brothers, who'd been lying in their sorry graves for better than ten years. He just wanted to get out the door and on his horse and on his way.

"Imagine that," Calvin said, his voice a monotone. "King Garner walkin' into my bar big as life. Must be fate or somethin'."

"Listen, Calvin, I've got no squawk with you," Garner said, and took a sideways step toward the door. "All that was a long time ago, and right now I'm—"

Without warning, Calvin swung a hogleg up from behind the bar and pulled the trigger, but not before Garner threw himself to the side. His gun skinned in midair, he got off two shots before he hit the floor.

One missed.

The other took Calvin in the shoulder.

Calvin screamed. He dropped that hogleg like it was on fire and, horrified, grabbed at his shoulder. "You shot me, you sonofabitch!" he cried, absolutely shocked that something like this could happen to a God's-on-my-side, righteous avenger like him. Garner had seen it before.

"Jesus Christ," Garner muttered in disgust. He

hauled himself up and took a quick look at Calvin before he scooped up the discarded hogleg.

"You shot me!" a hysterical Calvin wailed again. "Goddamn it, you shot me! I'm bleedin'!"

With a clatter, Garner tossed the hogleg to the other side of the room. He growled, "You point a gun at somebody, you're bound to get shot, you jackass," and punched the blustering Calvin in the jaw just as hard as he could.

Calvin dropped to the floor immediately, out cold.

"What's happenin'?" Pansy called from the top of the stairs. "Calvin? You all right?"

"He just hurt himself a little," Garner called back. "It's all right."

Garner was hurt, as well. Calvin's slug had creased his upper arm, and blood soaked his shirt. It wasn't a bad wound, but no wound was good.

Footsteps beat up the road. "Who's shootin'?" somebody called from outside. "Is there trouble?"

"What's goin' on in there?" called a second voice.

"Nothing," Garner said, stepping through the doors to find a small, ash-covered, panting crowd. As one, they took a step back when they saw him.

"Aw, calm down," he muttered. "Any of you folks see two strangers yesterday, just before the fire?"

"That butt-lickin' bastard killed old Jess and would'a killed Harry, too, if we hadn't got the door bashed down in time," said a man in a shirt that had once been blue, but was now streaked with soot and grime. He shook his fist. "He locked 'em in, then torched the livery. Ol' Jess never hurt a fly, and Harry, well, he's reformed. Ain't shot nobody in five or six years."

"Somebody else lived?" Garner asked. It was a day of miracles, all right, even if they were sideways ones.

"He's still breathin'," the man replied, "but barely. He's burnt up awful. Why would a stranger do somethin' so cruel?"

"That was Vince Martindale," Garner said, hoping that nobody out here was named Farley. "And there's no saying why he does what he does. He's just plain mean, from what I can figure. I'm tracking him and his partner."

Meekly, another man offered, "He burnt up my dry-goods store, too."

"And my house," spat another. "Murderin', home-wreckin' sonofabitch. Where are Martha and me gonna stay, mister? Where we gonna put the kids?"

"Hanging's too good for him," said the first man. "Lord, poor Harry and Jess." He wrapped his arms about himself and hugged his shoulders.

"Oughta do like the old days, back in England," said another. "Draw and quarter the skunk. Put his head on a pike!"

The first man said, "Aw, you don't even know what drawin' and quarterin' is, Frank."

The lone woman in the group, a handsome, blond gal with cornflower eyes and skirts blackened with soot, moved forward a little. She poked at the shoulder of the man who had just spoken, and said, "Jess is dead, Mr. Elvin, and all the bloodthirsty vengeance in the world won't bring him back." She pointed at Garner. "You're bleeding, sir."

"Yes, ma'am," he said, tipping his hat. "I know. Anybody see which way they rode out of town?"

Three men pointed up the street.

It was good enough for Garner.

"You the law?" asked Frank, the draw and quarter man.

"Sort of," Garner replied. He pulled down his water bag and filled it in the trough near the rail. The water was fairly clean at least, and just at the moment he didn't have time to find another source. "There'll likely be a U.S. deputy marshal through here tomorrow or the next day. Marcus Trevor's his name. Just send him on after me."

Like it will do him any good, Garner thought.

"Shouldn't someone see to your wound?" the woman with the cornflower eyes asked. There was an offer of more than wound-tending in there, and for just a half second, Garner was awfully tempted.

But he said, "Thank you, ma'am," then slung the full water bag back up and secured it. "I'll be fine."

He swung a leg over Faro and reined him around. "Somebody best see to Calvin, though," he said, nodding toward the bar. "Believe he had a little accident."

Garner followed Belasco and Martindale's trail for roughly two more miles before he stopped to make camp. Faro was tired, he was tired, and he supposed he should do something about his arm.

After he grained and watered Faro, he set about the business of doctoring himself. Once he got his shirt off, he found that he'd been right. The slug had cut a narrow channel across his flesh, nothing more. Not a bad wound at all, but it still stung like holy hell.

He bathed it as best he could, then ripped his new shirt, the one he'd bought in Phoenix, into strips, grumbling all the while. If he'd known he was going to have to rip it into bandages, he would have just bought a yard of cotton.

He set to wrapping his wound.

He wondered how Hobie was doing with those two numbskulls.

He wondered about the rental horse that they'd cut loose back down the trail. At least, Hobie had better have cut it loose, if he knew what was good for him.

He wondered where Martindale and Belasco had camped tonight, and how much farther he'd have to travel to catch them.

But mostly, he was just tired. So tired, in fact, that he fell into a sound sleep right where he sat, and didn't so much as make a fire or eat until the next morning.

11

Deputy Trevor, Hobie, and Woolsey had camped about ten miles east of High Draw. At least, that's what Trevor had told Hobie, who had never been down this way and knew exactly nothing about the topography.

Hobie knew, however, that ten miles over terrain like this traveled like twenty-five over smoother, more giving ground. Hilly, rocky, hard, and sere, that's what he was having to contend with. It wasn't like up north, back home, where there was forest and grassland, where a body moving through the trees bent twigs and beat down tender weeds, tore leaves from trees, and left the evidence of its passing in crushed pine needles or green moss skinned from stone.

Martindale and Belasco's tracks were still there, but growing more difficult to follow with every passing hour. Wind blew lazily at their tracks, which were faint to begin with. Animals crossed them. What little vegetation there was grew just a smidgen every day, and healed over slight wounds caused by the passing of their horses' hooves.

But there was still a trace, still enough, and he was on it like a snuffling hound dog, nose to the ground. They were lucky in that Martindale and Belasco seemed to be in no hurry. Hobie figured that despite the time-consuming task of trailing them, the men they were tracking had tarried enough that he and the deputy and Woolsey had gained about a day on them. Hobie thought that Garner would have been proud of him.

He was thinking about Garner a lot, lately. He imagined Garner was far ahead. At least, he hoped so. He sure hadn't seen any trace of Garner's track, and they'd come quite a way since he'd ridden off and left them.

But maybe Garner, who knew this country far better than he, had known about that town up there, and short-cutted to it. Maybe he already had Belasco and Martindale hog-tied. Maybe he was someplace ahead, someplace in the shade, waiting for them to catch up.

Then again, perhaps Garner had just washed his hands of the whole business and headed back north, cussing them the whole time. But if he had, why wouldn't he have taken Hobie with him?

It was a puzzlement.

It surely would be a laugh on Hobie if he'd done all this fancy tracking just to curry favor with Garner, and Garner wasn't even there to see it. Or at least, see the end result. And it would sure be a double-darned shame if after this was all over and he went back home, he returned to find Garner sitting out on the porch, drunk. Just like before.

Sighing, he slung his saddle blanket up on Fly, then hoisted the saddle into place.

"Reckon we'll make High Draw before nightfall,

fella," he said, reaching under the buckskin's belly for the girth. He ran the strap through the ring, then doubled it. "Mayhap you'll get to spend the night on a straw bed and under a roof, Fly. Mayhap I will, too. Course, I'm thinkin' about a feather mattress for myself."

He had just given the girth strap a final tug and tied it off when a hand fell on his shoulder and rudely shoved him aside.

He stumbled and half fell, but caught himself. It was that damned reporter! "What in tarnation are you doin', Woolsey?" he shouted.

Looking much the worse for several days of travel, Clive Woolsey stood beside Fly, one hand on the horn, his other guiding his foot toward the stirrup. "I won't ride that mule another day," he said, nose in the air. "You ride him. I'm taking this horse."

"Like spit you are," Hobie said, and pushed him away before he could shove his foot in the stirrup. "There's nothin' wrong with Charlie Blue."

"If there's nothing wrong with him, then why can't you ride him?" Woolsey sniffed.

Woolsey just plain didn't get the fact that Fly was Hobie's. Why, you'd think Woolsey figured every horse he saw was available to anyone who came along, like the whole world of horses was just some giant rental barn!

Hobie forced his anger down, though, and as calmly as he could, said, "You can't just take a feller's horse 'cause you want it. Don't work that way. And you wouldn't get dumped so much if you'd pay attention to what you were doin'."

Woolsey drew himself up. "Three times!" he cried. "Three times, just yesterday." He jabbed an accusing finger toward Charlie Blue. "This blasted creature is trying to kill me. I want a real horse."

Trevor, who had so far remained silent, dropped his stirrup down and swung a leg over his gray. He looked down at them and said, "You had you a real horse till the day before yesterday, there, Woolsey."

"Until you lamed it," Hobie added indignantly. "Any horse can pick up a stone bruise, but that one could'a been avoided. You pickin' out Charlie Blue's feet?"

Woolsey glowered.

Trevor smirked. "You're soundin' a whole lot like King, Hobie."

Hobie looked up. "I'll be takin' that as a compliment, Deputy."

"Wasn't meant no other way," Trevor replied.

Hobie poked a finger against Woolsey's chest. "And you stay away from my horse. Now get on your mule and let's go."

"Yessir," Hobie heard Trevor mutter as he reined his gray away. "Just like ol' King."

Belasco and Martindale were breaking camp, too.

Belasco was still kind of mad at him, Martindale thought dully, but tough turds, as his daddy used to say. It didn't diminish the way he still felt about that beautiful conflagration. It been one hell of a fire, all right. Bright, and excruciatingly painful. He wished he could have stayed around to see it take the town. As it was, he'd only gotten to glimpse the second and third buildings go up from a far-away hill's crest.

He should have put somebody in those other shacks, too, he'd thought belatedly. Somebody who would have hollered real loud, so he could have heard them from atop that distant hill.

He rolled up his bedding and tied it behind his saddle. Belasco was doing the same. Belasco always woke up hours before Martindale, shaved and washed and God knows what else—maybe drew things on his toenails or knitted tea cozies or trimmed the goddamn cactus for all Martindale knew. And then he woke Martindale with breakfast.

Not this morning, though. Sure, Belasco had been up when Martindale woke, but there'd been no breakfast. No coffee, not even any of those rotten fried biscuits of his. Nothing. And he hadn't so much as opened his mouth, not since the fire. Why, it made a fellow feel like some kind of outcast when even his partner wouldn't talk to him!

Oh, he'd tried getting Belasco to speak. "Mornin', Belasco," he'd said.

No reply.

"How's about some chuck?" he'd asked.

Silence.

"Like me to screw your mama?" he'd ventured.

Not a word. Not even a sock in the jaw. Martindale could have lived with either one.

Well, two could play the quiet game, he thought. If Belasco didn't want to talk to him, fine. Martindale thought he just might be able to think of a way to make ol' Donny holler. Belasco would wish he'd talked to him then, wouldn't he?

And Belasco was hurrying them all of a sudden. Why, after they'd killed those ranch folks outside Baker, they'd been riding along like it was a pleasure tour. But not anymore. Now it was push, push, push. Martindale didn't see why. High Draw didn't even have a sheriff, and those folks were probably still trying to put out the fire.

Smiling, he swung up on his horse, reached behind him and pried a chunk of ancient, molding jerky from the bottom of his saddlebag, and chewing, followed the silent Belasco northwest.

Clive Woolsey clung to the plodding mule like a starving tick, his arms and legs dug in every which way. He had come to think of his participation in this horrid little jaunt as having nothing to do with free will, and everything to do with impressed servitude.

Oh, he'd show them, once he got back to some vestige of civilization. He hadn't decided which was the best way to portray King Garner. At first, he thought he'd write Garner up as the "master tracker and celebrated manhunter" who'd abandoned them in the wilderness to pursue his own selfish pleasures, and therefore shown his true colors.

But then, he thought, perhaps master tracker and manhunter was too much credit to give Garner, even if Woolsey only planned to tear him down later. Perhaps he'd be best drawn as a worthless old has-been, deadweight that had dragged them down until they'd forced him to leave their company. Trevor had drawn his pistol, hadn't he? Woolsey would just have him aiming it at Garner rather than himself. The more he thought about it, it wasn't too much off the mark.

Yes, he liked that one best. At least for now. He might think of something better later on, though. Best to keep one's options open.

He'd decided that Deputy Trevor was an idiot. Oh, he'd known from the start that the man was out after the best—and the most—notoriety he could possibly get. He had stars in his eyes, and wanted fame, promotion, and possibly fortune. Naturally, this pursuit necessitated getting his name in the papers as much as possible, and linked to a sensational case.

Woolsey had known from the first that the deputy was using him. But then, wasn't it mutual? For the chance to get out of this barbaric country once and for all, he could—and would—write about goose shit and gravel so glowingly that his readers would think it was caviar and pearls.

And that little skunk's backside, Hobie! What sort of name was that for a grown man, anyway? Certainly, he was trailing these abominable ruffians with some degree of skill, but couldn't everyone out West do that as naturally as a native New Yorker could find a good restaurant? Woolsey had the distinct feeling that U.S. Deputy Marshal Trevor was only keeping Hobie on out of some sort of debt to Garner, although he didn't have the slightest idea what that debt might be.

Well, he'd tar Hobie Hobson with the same brush he planned to use on King Garner.

And this filthy mule!

Clive Woolsey, pick out hooves? Heaven forbid! He hadn't touched so much as a horse brush in all the time he'd been in Arizona, and he wasn't going to start being an equine nursemaid now. Let the damned mule clean his own feet. Better yet, let Deputy Trevor do it when he saddled the wretched beast each morning.

Woolsey had fallen a few lengths behind the others, and kicked Charlie Blue in the ribs. The mule took exception to this unexpected rudeness, and promptly thrust his head toward the ground and bucked out with his hind legs.

Woolsey didn't fall off, but his position aboard the mule was substantially altered.

"Need some help, there, Woolsey?" Trevor called to

him as he worked his way down the filthy beast's neck and back into the saddle.

Woolsey ground his teeth and slapped at his pocket to make sure he hadn't lost his notepad and lead pencil. But he didn't answer.

Belasco and Martindale's trail was easier to follow now, clearer and fresher, and they didn't appear to be taking any pains to hide it. Jack-sure little bastards, weren't they?

Garner rode along at a walk or a leisurely trot, according the terrain. He kept an eye to the brushy ground, and thanked his stars that Faro had such a good, soft jog. His wounded arm didn't need any more jarring than necessary.

He trailed Belasco and Martindale through low, rolling hills that were just seeing the first soft greens and tender wildflowers of spring, and the new broods of infant quail that darted through the undergrowth after their mamas. Then he followed them down onto the flat, where the vegetation grew sparse but pretty, then up in altitude again. Always, the trail led west, keeping well clear of the border. If they went too awful much further, he thought, they'd ride right back into Yuma Prison.

Garner shook his head. If he'd been Donny Belasco, he would have headed in the opposite direction and not stopped until he hit the Atlantic Ocean. Maybe not even then.

Of course, Garner wouldn't be surprised at any stunt that Martindale tried to pull off. He made a box of rocks look practically clever. The only reason he'd survived this long was that at some point, an innate animal cunning took over, and so far, it had saved his sorry ass every time. Martindale was a creature of instinct, not thought.

But Donny was a whole other matter.

Marcus Trevor had fed him a line of horseshit back up at the ranch, and Garner knew it. Belasco wasn't out to get him. Garner figured Donny hadn't thought of him once since he'd hauled him in and testified up in Prescott. Belasco was too driven, too focused.

Too crazy.

However, Garner would have been delighted if Belasco had set his sights on him when he broke out. It sure would have saved a lot of lives. Garner could have stayed home in comfort, set a trap, and taken the little sonofabitch out—permanently—when he came to call. But Garner wasn't Belasco's meat, not by a long shot.

At the trial there'd been some talk of the newfangled scientific sort, about Belasco's boyhood and what had turned him this way. Garner couldn't remember most of it anymore. He thought it was crud then, and he still thought so.

He recalled some of Martindale's background, though. Something about how his daddy, a half-Mexican, half-English farmer, had gone peach-orchard crazy one day and tried to burn him and his baby sister up in the cabin. They said the sister had died. Martindale carried around the burns to this day.

Still, it didn't seem any excuse at all.

Hell, when Garner was six or thereabouts, he'd fallen from the barn's hayloft and broken his leg and both his arms, and just about killed himself to boot. He didn't go around tossing people off roofs, did he?

He'd done some bad things during the war, and some bad things after. He'd admit to that. But he liked to think that on the whole, he'd lived a fairly good life.

He'd helped a few people. Course, that was by his count, not the Lord's. Just because a fellow didn't go round killing for the fun of it didn't mean that the Creator was going to set a gold crown on his head when the time came. Garner had a feeling the Lord was a lot stricter than that.

And Garner was about to do a killing. Two killings if he had the chance, and pretty soon by the looks of these tracks. Not for fun, of course, but for what? Vengeance? Honor? Just to uphold his own private sense of right and wrong?

Garner figured it didn't much matter. By his book, these killings had to be done, and a killing was a killing, after all. Anyway you looked at it, somebody ended up dead.

He wondered just how fine a point God put on that Sixth Commandment.

Or maybe it was the Seventh.

He gave his head a shake. "I'm goin' loony," he muttered, glaring out into space. "Thinkin' like a damn preacher!"

One way or the other, he was going to do what he had to. And he supposed the Good Lord would, too.

12

"Aw, crud," **Hobie** whispered once he got his first look at High Draw.

Trevor rode up beside him and looked down at the ruined town below. He whistled, long and drawn out. "You're not foolin', kid," he said quietly, and thumbed back his hat. "Martindale's been here or I'm a monkey's uncle."

"What?" said Woolsey, who was just catching up to them on the lagging Charlie Blue. "What is it?" And then he saw. "Dear God," he whispered. Then he seemed to think of something, and his lips pursed. "This is King Garner's fault."

With a complaint of saddle leather, Hobie twisted toward him. "You gone crazy? Crazier than usual, I mean?"

Woolsey made an effort to sit up straighter in the saddle, although he was still fairly hunched over the horn. "It's Garner's fault. Deputy Trevor has mentioned at least three times what an excellent tracker the man is. If he had stayed with us, perhaps we would have caught up with these blasted ruffians before they perpetrated this heinous—"

"Oh, shut up," Trevor grumbled, and moved his gray on down the hill before Woolsey could finish his sentence.

Hobie was right behind him. It looked to him as if a good three quarters of the town was in rubble. The only things left were a saloon and two houses, one of which had a placard out front welcoming boarders. This sign had a large red X painted through it, and another, larger sign tacked underneath stating, "Full Full Full!"

Any hopes of a feather mattress fled his mind. By the looks of the crowd on the porch, the whole town was tripled or quadrupled up in there. Heck, they were probably sleeping five to a bed and six across on the floors.

At the base of a hill to the north of town, they seemed to be holding a funeral. At least, there were a lot of folks gathered up there, and most of them seemed to be dressed in black. Course, Hobie thought, that just might be from putting out the fire. . . .

"Deputy Trevor?" he said.

"Yeah, I see 'em," Trevor replied, and reined his gray toward the group.

It was indeed a funeral, although Hobie had been only three-quarters right about the clothing. The three dismounted a respectful distance back from the throng, ground-tied their mounts, and made their way up the slope.

The service was breaking up about then, and folks were coming toward them. In the distance, Hobie could see the grave diggers filling in the hole.

"Howdy, ma'am," Trevor said, tipping his hat to the

first person who walked down from the cemetery. "Might I ask who's in charge around here?"

The woman blinked. "Jason Thread, I suppose," she said. Her voice was heavy, although more with exhaustion than grief, Hobie guessed. She didn't look to have been crying.

The woman turned and pointed, her dark shawl fanning beneath her arm like a bat's wing. "Back there. Black suit, plaid shirt. He's the mayor."

Trevor tipped his hat again. "I thank you kindly, ma'am."

She turned to leave, then stopped. "You the federal deputy?" she asked.

Trevor nodded.

"About damn time," she said wearily, and walked off without another word.

"I'll be," mused Trevor.

"'It is Deputy Trevor, come to save us!'" quoted Woolsey, presumably from the article he had yet to write. His eyes were lifted to the heavens.

"You got a way with words, there, Woolsey," Trevor said, and started on up the hill again.

Hobie and Woolsey scurried after.

Garner had made good time. Martindale and Belasco were hurrying now, as if they knew they were being pursued. Well, not quite. They were taking no pains whatsoever to cover their trail, which was fine with Garner. Martindale and Belasco were fast, but not as fast he was. He figured he'd picked up another hour on them, maybe two.

Maybe more.

The land he was tracking them through had been, since noon, a low, flattish desert, covered in sand and gravel and clay, with a few paloverde trees, which were laden with yellow spring bloom. His path was thick with bristly cholla, creosote, barrel cactus, and yucca, in addition to the usual desert scrub and spring flowers.

Martindale and Belasco had made a wide, sloppy path right through it, crushing tender flowers, snapping branches off bushes, circling wide around the cholla. They'd busted up enough creosote that he could have tracked them by smell alone. Even if they hadn't, he could have tracked them from a half mile off, their path was that plain.

This day, he hadn't given so much as a thought to the whys and wherefores of what he was doing. He had fallen into old habits, old patterns, tracking for the sake of tracking, trailing wanted men just because they needed to be tracked. He was like a hound with his nose on a warm trail, enjoying the hunt.

Smiling, he rode on.

Woolsey was just plain disgusted.

He'd been sitting here for the past hour, sipping a warm beer just to be sociable, and listening to this confounded claptrap when they ought to be on their way!

The bartender was trying to press a claim against King Garner for the murder of his cousins—who, Woolsey gathered from Trevor's attitude, had it coming to them—and for shooting *him*. Cold-blooded, the bartender claimed it was, much the same as the murder of his cousins.

And he claimed that he, himself, had been unarmed.

This, too, Trevor pooh-poohed.

But it was clear that, Trevor's previous assurances asides, Garner hadn't gone home at all. He was still on the trail. And worse, he was a good day's ride ahead of them.

"Hush up, Calvin Farley," said a woman with striking cornflower-blue eyes. Nearly the entire populace—men, women, children, some stray poultry, and three dogs—was in the bar, and they were all trying to speak at once. But when this particular woman stood up and spoke, every last man jack of them quieted. She continued, "This Mr. Garner seemed a very nice man. We all heard three shots, and we all saw where you'd wounded him. So just hold your tongue."

She sat down again, and the room resumed its buzzing.

"Still say you oughta catch him and string him up," Calvin said sullenly.

"Farley, you say?" said Trevor, his brows arched. He stared at the bartender. "That explains a lot."

Woolsey tipped his head. Hadn't Deputy Trevor mentioned this name before in one of those endless diatribes about Famous Outlaws He Had Brought to Justice?

"Farley?" he repeated. "Didn't you tell me that you—"

"Never mind," Trevor interrupted.

"—brought in the Farley brothers?" Woolsey finished.

"Uh, Garner helped," said Trevor.

Hobie set his lips, for what reason Woolsey couldn't imagine, and piped up, "Deputy, they already told us that Martindale and Belasco were here. Hadn't we best get—"

Trevor waved his hand. "Not yet, Hobie," he said, just as one of the woman fawningly pressed a plate of cold fried chicken on him. "Why, thank you, ma'am," he said, doffing his hat momentarily. She blushed. "Don't mind if I do." He offered the plate. "Boys?"

Reluctantly, Hobie took a drumstick, but he appeared distracted and upset. He kept looking toward the doors, toward the waning afternoon light, and that drumstick went *thump-thump-thump* on the tabletop, leaving greasy marks on the scarred wood.

Little Hobie might be a pipsqueak, Woolsey grudgingly admitted to himself, but he certainly had more brains than Trevor, who seemed to have entirely forgotten about the murderers. He had nothing on his mind except drinking in the town folks' adulation. And, it seemed, gladly taking credit for every outlaw capture in the Territory since a time five or ten years before his birth.

Give him another five minutes, Woolsey thought, and he'll be signing autographs.

Of course, Trevor could probably sign those autographs George Armstrong Custer and no one would be the wiser. These people must be a sorry lot if this was their idea of a famous man. Why, none of them even knew Trevor's name! The only thing they knew was that he was a federal man, and that he was telling them a lot of tall tales that they took to be true.

Since Trevor didn't appear to be coming down out of the clouds any time soon, Woolsey turned to one of the men crowded around their table and said, "This young woman. The one who lived through Belasco's . . . intentions. Is she still here?"

The man glanced over his shoulder, then pointed to a thin, wan, bandaged girl—only in her teens—peering over the banister from the second floor. "That's Pansy," he said.

"Thank you," said Woolsey with a curt nod, and pulling his notepad from his pocket, stood up.

"I think we oughta leave, that's all," Hobie said.

"Don't be so damned uppity, kid," Marcus Trevor replied, and lit his cigarette. He shook out the match and tossed it, still smoking feebly, into the dark street. "We'll go soon enough."

"And you'd best stop taking credit for things you didn't do."

Trevor arched a brow. "Like what, for instance?"

"Like bringin' in the Farley brothers. Like leadin' the Army to Geronimo right before he got sent to Florida. Like—"

"All right, all right, I get your point," Trevor said. "You can't blame a fellow for braggin' just a little when he's got such a good audience, though."

"A little?" Hobie asked.

Trevor blew out a hazy plume and gazed up at the honeyed moon, hanging low in the sky. "'Sides," he went on, "we can't leave tonight. It's dark. Ain't nobody can track in the dark."

"I can," said Hobie, quietly defiant. "There's that great big fat moon up there, near full. There's plenty of light to track, honest. We were gainin' on 'em, Deputy Trevor, and now you want to stay till tomorrow afternoon!" He was afraid that the last bit had come out on the whiny side, and shut his mouth before he made it any worse.

Trevor didn't seem to notice, though. In a voice meant to be convincing, he said, "Now, Hobie, a half day ain't gonna matter one way or t'other. And these nice folks have offered to fix us a real Sunday dinner. Throw us a party, like. Be a shame to disappoint—"

"Dang it, Deputy!" Hobie interrupted. "I ain't stupid, you know. You wanted me to track for you and I been doin' it good, ain't I? But if I have got to listen to you tell one more of those dad-gum, fluffed-up, outright-lie-packed stories about how you settled the West single-handed, I swear, I'm gonna shoot you myself."

Trevor blinked.

Hobie blushed hot enough that he was sure Trevor could see it, then hurriedly said, "I, uh . . . Sorry." He hadn't meant it to be such an outburst. But the truth was, he'd followed Garner because he wanted to witness some real heroics before the time for them was gone, and when Deputy Trevor had hitched up to them, he'd thought he'd be in for a double treat.

But so far, Garner was the only one who'd done anything remotely herolike. Hobie counted Garner's walking into the Cartwell house (and not throwing up when he came out) as one incident, and telling Deputy Trevor to find his own damned fugitives by himself (then going out alone to bring them to justice) as the other.

And Trevor had done exactly nothing except talk himself up and admire himself in his shaving mirror. Several of those deeds he was bragging up to Woolsey, why, Hobie knew for an actual fact had been done by other men, and at least one of them—the Farley capture—had been done by none other than King Garner, and all by his lonesome! Trevor usually told the wilder ones to Woolsey when he thought that Hobie couldn't hear, but Hobie had better ears than Trevor suspected. And Hobie's patience was wearing thin.

Trevor remained silent, smoking his cigarette.

"Sorry," Hobie repeated. "But to be plain truthful, Deputy, your star has taken a dip with me."

Brows knitted, Trevor glanced at his badge.

"No," said Hobie, "I meant . . . Never mind."

"Kid," said Trevor, grinding the butt of his smoke under his heel, "I'm with King. I just don't understand how your brain works. And for your information," he continued, his voice growing stern, "that Woolsey fellow asked me to tell about myself. For that article he's writin'. If I been exaggeratin' a tad here and there, it's just to make a good story."

He stopped for a moment and stared at Hobie, his eyes narrowed. "You know, I think you're jealous 'cause he ain't asked you beans."

Hobie rolled his eyes. "You'll pardon me for sayin' it, Deputy, but I think you've drunk too much free booze tonight." And before Trevor could think of a good retort, Hobie tipped his hat and added, "I'm goin' to bed down, now. It's been a real long day."

Hobie turned and walked away, toward where the horses were tethered. And as he did, he heard Trevor's gruff mutter, "Least the little shit's right about that."

Garner had camped in a sheltered place where yellow rocks jutted ten and twelve feet high, as jagged as an old dog's teeth. The terrain had grown increasingly rougher as the day wore on. Much more of this and Martindale and Belasco would be up in the hills again, with him after them.

He'd gained a good bit on those boys today, all right, Garner thought as he rubbed down Faro. For an animal who hadn't been out on the hunt for over two years, the horse was holding up just fine. Garner went over the gelding's feet several times a day, and each night he felt all four legs from hoof to elbow, checking for tendons beginning to bow and the like.

Despite what Woolsey thought—if, in fact, he ever

thought about anything at all besides his damned story—out here, a man was only as good as the mount that carried him.

"So far, so good, buddy," he said as he reached Faro's head.

The bay whickered and shoved at him with his nose.

"Yeah, yeah," Garner said, smiling, and started on the other side of the horse.

He had already built a fire and started the coffee to heating and the beans to soaking. Another day, he thought, and he might have them.

Or not. Martindale and Belasco were slowly turning northward, for what reason Garner couldn't fathom. And if they kept on turning, they'd miss Yuma entirely.

That would be a big plus in the mind of any other man, but not, he guessed, to Donny Belasco. The only thing that seemed to count to Belasco was to get to another place where there were women. Yuma sure had plenty of those.

Had Martindale talked him out of it?

Again, highly unlikely.

So why were they all of a sudden swinging north?

By three o'clock in the morning, Hobie was still lying awake in his bedroll, staring up at the stars. He was alone out here with the horses, for the town folk had offered the deputy a bed. And where Trevor went, Woolsey followed, his notebook in hand, that stub of lead pencil at the ready.

He thought about Garner out there, all alone, nose to the trail, doing all the work.

He thought about Trevor, who, for all he knew, was still awake, expounding on the deeds of great men and calling them his own while that snotty-nosed scribbler wrote down his every word.

Schoolboy, my butt, he thought, grinding his teeth.

He sat up.

There was less light now than before, the moon having moved high up in the sky and shrunk a good bit. But there was still enough light to trail by if a fellow was handy and knew where to look.

He'd catch up with Garner, and he didn't give a flying fig whether that glory seeking Trevor and his pal ever got there or not. Let them sit around and eat fried chicken and brag all week, for all he cared. While they were lounging around in the saloon, he'd see what real heroics were, by gum.

Quietly, he rolled his bedding up tight and saddled old Fly. "You up for a little adventure?" he whispered to the buckskin as he fastened the girth strap. "You up for gettin' a taste of genuine bravery?"

Fly didn't do anything more than snort, but Hobie took it for a yes.

For a moment he hesitated, then pinned his deputy badge to Stealth's halter, where he was certain Trevor would see it.

He mounted up and slowly, by the light of the moon, made his way up the street and out of town.

13

"**Tell me why** we're goin this way again?" Martindale asked. Belasco was speaking to him this morning, but Martindale wasn't sure he liked the change.

"Because I wish to," Belasco answered curtly, never taking his eyes off the horizon.

"Goddamn it, that ain't no answer!" Martindale huffed.

This time, Belasco turned in the saddle and looked him straight in the eye. "It's all I'm prepared to give you, my friend." He didn't smile.

"You're sure makin' me sore at you," Martindale said with a growl.

"Ditto," replied Belasco and turned away.

"Quit talkin' foreign languages at me all the time!" Martindale railed, angrier than ever. "I ain't as stupid as you think."

Belasco reined in his horse. "Really, Vincent? Why, you certainly had me fooled."

Martindale jerked his mount to a halt as well. "God-damn it!" he shouted. "Get down! Get off that horse right now!"

Belasco cocked his head. "Whatever for?"

"Because I'm gonna slug you so hard your grand-kids'll be born dizzy, that's why."

Belasco closed his eyes for a moment. "Vincent, think. I know it's difficult, but try. I fear that your fiery little display back in High Draw will have attracted quite a bit of adverse attention. Quite a bit more, I should like to point out, than the death—in this case, just the wounding—of a prostitute. And that we may, at this very moment, be being trailed by officers of the law. Now, wouldn't we be foolish to waste our time in fisticuffs when we could be traveling?"

It was a good bit of information for Martindale to di-gest all at once, and rather than try to figure it out, he leaned toward Belasco and said, "Ha!"

Belasco made a face and pulled his head back. "Your breath, Vincent. Please."

"That's another thing," Martindale crowed as Be-lasco started his horse moving again. Martindale kicked his horse to catch up. "You shut up about my breath and my not takin' baths and stuff. You waste a whole lot of water. Somebody has to make up the difference, you fancy-ass sonofabitch, or we'd die of thirst. Besides, this ain't some slicked up drawin' room we're in out here."

"Well, you certainly hit that nail on the head," Be-lasco said, although he didn't look over.

Martindale dropped back a little and worked his jaw back and forth over teeth that didn't appreciate the ef-fort. He didn't like all this nastiness that was coming from his partner any more than he'd liked the silence he'd gotten all day yesterday.

Belasco was getting to be a real pain in the ass. Maybe Martindale would just put into action all those things he'd been dreaming up to do to him. Course, just one of them would kill the highfalutin bastard.

The thought made him smile, and more softly, he said, "I reckon one of us is gonna end up dead, Belasco."

"Probably," came the disinterested reply.

It was a shame there wasn't any wood good enough for burning out here, but a feller had to make do in a pinch. Martindale eased his gun from its holster and cocked it, aimed it at Belasco's back.

At the sound, Belasco started to turn, saying, "What is it now, Vincent?"

Martindale fired.

Belasco fell off his horse with a resounding thump, more of a thump than you'd think a skinny fellow could make, and lay still.

Martindale just sat there, staring at him for a good couple of minutes, trying to decide whether he should root through his saddlebags or take his horse or both. Finally, he decided just to leave everything.

Hell, he was liable to run into a string full of hooker's ears, and he didn't believe he could stomach that.

"Keep your stuff, you sick bastard," he said, and then he spat on the body.

Martindale holstered his gun and went on his way, leaving Belasco behind on the open plain, his horse standing over him.

Deputy Trevor slept in.

They'd given him and Woolsey a whole room all to themselves over at the boardinghouse. He'd counted eight bedrolls taken out to accommodate them, plus he figured the bed could have held three more, if you packed them in tightly enough. Poor devils were probably sleeping out on the porch.

No, he corrected himself. The porch was already full.

Well, good sleeping arrangements when you got to a town were part of the job, one of the perks. So was sleeping until nine-thirty in the morning. He was sure looking forward to that Sunday dinner the town had promised him. He hoped it would be barbecue or at least a big roast. He'd eaten almost a whole chicken last night, and he was sick of chicken for the time being. Licking his lips, he sat up and rubbed at his eyes, then gave Woolsey a little kick.

"I'm up, drat it, I'm up," said Woolsey from the floor.

"Open your eyes, then," Trevor said. He stood up and stretched his arms, then stepped over the prone Woolsey to get to his clothes and personal items. He poured water into the basin on the dresser, took an adoring look in the mirror, then splashed his face and lathered it.

"Y'know," he said rather grandly, stropping his razor, "this reminds me of the time I was tracking Arlo Summers through red rock country. I came to this little mite of a town, not any bigger than this one, and—"

Eyes still closed, Woolsey lifted a hand and waved it. "Stop," he said. "It's too early to write anything down."

"Oh," said Trevor. He was more than a little disappointed.

"I could sleep another six hours," Woolsey went on, "even if I had to continue on this wretched floor."

"Beats rocks and dirt, don't it?" Trevor replied, and tilted his chin to get at his throat.

Behind him, Woolsey sat up. "Where's our little

friend?" he asked conversationally. "Still out with the horses?"

"Yup," Trevor said. "Guess he was a little mad, what with me taking these kind folks up on their invite to dinner and all. He wanted to go on out after 'em last night, if you can believe that."

Woolsey climbed to his feet, placed his hands in the small of his back, and stretched. Lank hair hung damply in eyes deprived of glasses. He took a step toward the nightstand and began to feel for them. "If he thought he could see well enough to track them," Woolsey said, settling the spectacles on his nose, "I believe we should have, Deputy."

Trevor wheeled, nearly slicing his cheek. "Listen, who's in charge here?"

Woolsey scowled a little, but held up both his hands, palms out. "My apologies. I thought that since our purpose in being out in the forsaken middle of nowhere was to catch these criminals, and since Hobie apparently felt he could track them, as well as Mr. Garner—who will now most probably make the arrests—it would have behooved us to—"

"You wanna get left off here?" Trevor growled before he thought better of it. He softened a little. "Listen, Clive, I know what I'm doin'. Those boys ain't gonna get away from us, I can promise you that. Hobie ain't never been on a manhunt before. He doesn't understand how things work. And King can't take those two all by his lonesome. He'll find 'em, but he'll wait for us to back him up."

He stopped a moment, his mouth working almost imperceptibly. "You wait and see," he added, more to talk himself into it than to convince Woolsey. Suddenly, he was a little worried.

"I see," said Woolsey with a nod. He began to put on his clothes.

Little bastard, thought Trevor, and returned to his mirror, scowling. But abruptly, he smiled. God, he was a handsome man, wasn't he? Good thing there weren't many mirrors on the trail, or he could spend all his time looking into one. Annie said he was the vainest man she'd ever known.

That Annie! What a card.

Garner would wait. Of course he would.

Both men were dressed and shaved before they went downstairs, and as soon as Trevor shook a few hands and kissed a baby—and determined that beef was indeed on the menu for their dinner—he and Woolsey wandered down the street.

"Bet Hobie's fit to be tied, us sleepin' in so late," Trevor remarked.

Woolsey made no comment.

Until they got a tad further down the road, that is. Then he stopped and pointed.

"Where's his horse?" he asked.

"That's funny," said Trevor. Then he gave a shrug. "Oh, he's probably gone to take a look at the track. He'll be back in plenty of time for dinner. He's a growin' boy, y'know."

But when they stopped inside the saloon, the first thing out of Pansy's mouth—for she was downstairs today, bandaged head and all—was, "Where'd you send that kid a'yours off to, Deputy? He goin' for reinforcements?"

"Beg pardon?" Trevor asked.

"He rode outta here in the middle of the night," she said. "I was up, and I seen him out my window. We all been wondering where you sent him to."

Behind her, four men in the crowd nodded their heads. "You send him back to Baker, did you, Deputy?" one asked.

Trevor recovered beautifully, he thought. "Yes," he said, stepping forcefully on Woolsey's toe, "sent him for more men. And I wanted to tell you all that as much as Mr. Woolsey, here, and I appreciate the offer of a good feed, we've gotta be on our way." Then theatrically, he added, "When evil is on the scout, the U.S. Marshals Service isn't far behind."

"You didn't have to step on my foot," Woolsey grumbled as he limped quickly back toward the boardinghouse, behind Trevor. "And that last remark you spewed at them didn't make any sense. Would you care to—"

"Shut up," Trevor hissed. "Just shut up and grab your things and let's get the hell out of here."

Hobie had made better time during the night than he'd dreamt possible. He'd kept his nose to Garner's tracks, fresh over the ones that Martindale and Belasco had left. They stood out like they'd been painted in bright red, they were that clear to him.

Before dawn, he had stopped for a little nap and to rest Fly a little, and been up again by six and on the trail.

It was one o'clock in the afternoon or a little after right now, and he'd stopped to rest Fly, his second such stop since dawn. Garner had taught him well. "A man alone in the open country needs to take better care of his horse than himself, kid, if he wants to see civilization again," Garner had said once, and Hobie had remembered.

Of course, Garner had said it quite a long time ago,

before he fell into the bottle. But he'd said a number of pithy things like that, and Hobie had salted them away, just in case.

He wondered if Garner, somewhere up ahead, had already cornered Martindale and Belasco. He wondered if he'd said one of those heroic-book things like, "Throw down your arms, or I shall execute you where you stand, evildoers!"

He sort of doubted it, though.

He checked his pocket watch. One-ten. Long enough.

He patted Fly's neck and tightened the girth again, lifted and gave a cursory look to each hoof, and stuck his foot in the stirrup.

"Don't use up all the glory by yourself, Boss," he muttered as he swung into the saddle. "Anyways, don't use it all up while there's nobody there to see."

He clucked softly to Fly, and the horse eased into a jog.

Slowly, Belasco regained consciousness. The desert wobbled before him at first, its pale greens as blurred as if seen through water and its tan, clay floor rising and falling softly.

But eventually, it all began to hold still, and when it did, the first thing he did after he sat up was to check his watch.

It hadn't been shattered in the fall, thank God, and the hands read one-thirteen. He hadn't been out a half hour.

Carefully, he climbed to his feet, steadied himself with one hand on the saddle, and said, "Good boy, stout fellow."

He didn't much care for horses, but he had the sense

to know that if this one had wandered off, his goose would surely have been cooked.

His back was incredibly sore, and slowly, he peeled off his jacket and shirt. Beneath, he was swathed in plates of painted metal.

One read "Murchison's Apparel," and was tied across his front from his waist to just above his nipples. The second, which he now eased away, was strapped across his back and read "Camden's Ague Remedy: World's Finest." It was also punctured, slightly to one side, by a jagged, roundish hole circled around by a large dent that had taken the brunt of the impact, and had made that shot feel like a hard blow to his back.

He let the signs drop to the dirt, then felt gingerly at his back.

He cried out when he first touched the bullet wound. The signs, which he had picked up in Tucson, had served him well. The sad little whore he'd killed there must have collected them, because there was a stack of them—rusted and obviously cast away—in her corner. Belasco had been suspicious of Martindale even then.

A good thing, too.

He closed his eyes, unconsciously squeezing his facial features into a grimace, as he dug fingers into the wound. The sign had served its purpose, for he didn't have to dig a quarter inch into his flesh before his gently groping fingers found the bullet.

He wedged his nail against it and popped the slug out, grunting loudly. New pain coursed through him. He imagined that if he'd been able to see his back, he would have seen the beginnings of a great, black bruise from below his shoulder blades to his waist.

"Better that than dead," he muttered through

clenched teeth, and then he started going through his saddlebags for alcohol and rags.

Fifteen minutes later, he had washed and bandaged himself, strapped the signs on again, and was slipping carefully into his shirt and jacket once more.

And all he could think about was that bastard of a brigand, Martindale, and what he was going to do to him.

14

Martindale had slowed his pace considerably, now that he didn't have Donny Belasco to worry about anymore. He fretted that he'd been too quick to get rid of him, though. Seemed a shame not to burn him, not to get to hear him holler.

And, oh, he would have hollered real pretty, wouldn't he?

Martindale smiled, then scowled. Damn it, anyhow! He should have thought about it a little longer before he let his temper get the best of him.

But no. There wasn't any timber for miles, nothing to get a fire even sparked up good, let alone burning hot enough for the time it took to kill a man, then cook him.

Maybe he'd done the right thing after all.

And then he topped the ridge he'd been riding up, and looked down into the sere valley below.

A house! A goddamn house! It was adobe, by the looks of it, but there was a shitter, and by God, it was wood.

Of all the rotten luck. Why, if he'd just put a cork in his temper for a couple of hours longer, he could have had his cake and eaten it, too. Or maybe it was eat his cake and have it. He could never remember.

Grinding his teeth, he rode down toward the house. It was long deserted by the look of it, its roof caved in and its walls slowly crumbling, but it might make a nice shelter for the night. Of course, it was a little early to think about stopping, but that damned Belasco had been pushing them so hard the last couple of days that he felt like he deserved a short day in the saddle.

He rode down into what had once been the yard, and tethered his horse. The house was a holy wreck, all right, and was older than spit. Whoever had built it probably fell to Apaches back in the old days, because the north and west sides of it were all scorched, like somebody had tried to burn them out. That was likely what had taken the roof. He found a couple of arrowheads in the dirt, and stuck in the rotted, fragile wood of the outhouse, too.

Well, shelter was shelter.

He tossed a few ancient, brittle tumbleweeds over a low-melted wall of the house, checked the rubble-strewn floor for rattlers and scorpions—he squashed one of the latter with a satisfied grin—and made himself at home.

Garner was close. He'd made up even more time on Martindale and Belasco this day. He supposed he was far ahead of Trevor and his crew by this time. Oh, he could just see Trevor, relaxing in a golden glow of hero worship back in High Draw. He'd seen some of these federal boys in action before. Trevor had likely ridden in there, all hair and badge and glory, and was likely taking credit for everything from winning the Civil War up to and including ending the Apache Wars and settling the West.

If, indeed, it could be considered settled.

Garner didn't think so. There was always some jackass or other out to bring back the "good" old days, and they always seemed to come to Arizona to do it.

It crossed his mind that he never would have been burdened by Marcus Trevor if, all those years ago, Donny Belasco hadn't started his killing spree in San Francisco, then worked down the California coast, then across the Colorado River into Arizona. That trail of blood crossing the California line made Donny's capture the business of the federal marshal's office.

Of course, Marcus had been pretty wet behind the ears when it first happened. Garner didn't even know if he'd been with the marshal's office back then. Probably not. He would have been in his early twenties then, wouldn't he?

But whether he'd been the property of the U.S. Marshals Service or not, it had been Garner who'd tracked Belasco down. Just some sheriff from over at Medicine Rock, just some nobody.

Frankly, most of the time he wished it had stayed that way.

Just some nobody.

The rocks had slowly petered out, and he found himself riding across a vast plain, peppered with flowering cactus and scrub. The tracks were exceptionally clear here, as clear as they'd been yesterday, and he eased Faro into a lope.

Along about at four in the afternoon, he came to something curious. He rode around the site, then dismounted and ground-tied Faro.

Something real interesting had happened here, all right. The two had stopped, and one had gone on alone. The second one had lain here for some time, with his horse standing over him. He'd likely been shot, Garner thought as he crouched down. Drops of blood spattered the soil in a few places, and Garner picked up a spent slug from the dirt. Looked like it had hit something that had practically squashed it, too. Curious.

Whichever of them had been hit had been down for a while, but he'd gotten back up and ridden after the other one. His fresher tracks overlaid the first set.

Garner scratched at his head. He doubted that there was anybody else out here tracking these sonsofbitches. So that left either Martindale shooting Belasco or Belasco shooting Martindale.

Now, just who did the deed?

Whoever he was, he wasn't too good a shot, if his victim had just gotten back up and climbed on his horse. But then, neither man was exactly known for his talent with a gun.

Garner watered Faro and took a gulp himself. It was getting late. He figured to have about fifteen minutes— a half hour, tops—of decent tracking time left to him. There was a moon, all right, and a clear sky, but he'd been going since dawn and he wasn't as young as he used to be.

That wound would have slowed at least one of them up considerably. And Garner wouldn't want to be the shooter when the victim caught up to him.

He decided to travel on for another quarter hour or so, then stop and make camp. Let them finish each other off. He'd be obliged.

•   •   •

"Where are we?" Woolsey asked for probably the fiftieth time. "I thought you were supposed to be a tracker of—and I quote you, I have it written down somewhere—'surpassing skill'!"

Trevor took a deep breath, then ground his teeth. "Shut up," he hissed through them. "I'll find it, damn you."

"That little idiot Hobie would have found it," Woolsey insisted. "He never would have lost it in the first place!"

"Shut up, I said," Trevor snapped. "Wasn't it you who was mouthin' off about Hobie from the time I let you come along?"

"That was before I realized what a superior trailsman he actually was," Woolsey sniffed. "He will be highly noted in my article."

Thinking the blackest of thoughts, Trevor stared at the ground again. It had to be here somewhere. "Screw you," he said to Woolsey, then veered out once again to the right, his eyes cast down to the desert gravel.

"Very clever," said Woolsey sarcastically. "I'll wager you're the comedic star of the U.S. Marshals Service. And it's getting late, you realize. We're going to have to stop for the night."

"I know it, dammit!" shouted Trevor, and then he saw something in the fading light. Had those pebbles been disturbed, those rocks turned over? And there, wasn't that some brush that had been disturbed? The light was going fast, and he had to ride right up on top of the place to see it decent.

Well, God bless America! he thought with sudden satisfaction. They'd come through here after all and he'd found the trail again, by God! Relief coursed through him like an icy wash through his bowels.

They'd been turning in circles for nearly an hour, and he'd been certain he'd lost the track for good. And that wouldn't do, wouldn't do at all, especially since he had that damned reporter with him. Hell, it would have ruined him!

"If you've lost their trail, I don't suppose it's beyond you to find some sort of a town?" Woolsey said. "Preferably one with a railroad station."

Damn snotty little bastard.

"Ain't lost it," Trevor said in a voice meant to be condescending, although he was concerned that it came out more relieved than anything else. "It's right here. And get off your mule. We're gonna make camp."

Woolsey's head jerked. "You don't mean to tell me!" he said.

"Just did," replied Trevor, and swung down off Stealth.

"My apologies, Deputy," Woolsey said with questionable sincerity. But at least he said it. He scrambled off Charlie Blue and doffed his silly little hat, which Charlie Blue immediately grabbed. Woolsey wrested it back. Wiping it on his sleeve, he added, "I bow to your superior tracking skills."

"You'd better," Trevor grumbled beneath his breath, and then, in a louder voice, said, "And you'd better watch that mule. You bring any of that fried chicken from High Draw?"

Woolsey ducked, just missing being clamped between Charlie Blue's yellow teeth. "I thought you did," he said. "Damn you, mule!"

Donny Belasco had left his horse tethered down at the bottom of the slope and crawled back up to the top on his belly.

It was dark now, had been for a while, but still he watched the wreck of a house through the spyglass. Martindale was in there, all right. He could see him plainly through a spot where there wasn't any wall. Martindale had built a fire on the floor of the house, and he was having his supper. While it was cooking he'd hummed, and Donny had heard it clear up here.

Martindale's sense of pitch was as foul as his halitosis.

Belasco bided his time. He would let Martindale finish his meal and bed down for the night. If possible, he'd let him go all the way to sleep. And then, he'd come a-creeping, come a-creeping with his little razor.

"Eat quickly, you back-shooting animal," Donny Belasco muttered. "Eat quickly, Vinnie, dear, and enjoy your meal," he added with a faint smile.

"Boss?"

Garner cracked his eyelids open to find Hobie—and Hobie's horse—standing over him. It took him half a second to take in the situation, and another half to shoot to his feet, or rather, his haunches. When he'd been sleeping for any time whatsoever, all the threats and money in the world couldn't get his joints to cooperate that fast.

"Trevor and that little peckerwood with you?" he asked hoarsely, twisting his head from side to side.

"Nope," Hobie replied, and swung down off Fly. "They're a good half day behind me, more if Deputy Trevor tracks like he brags."

Garner snorted.

"I gave the badge back," Hobie said.

"I should hope to kiss a pig, you did," replied Garner somewhat gruffly. He was actually relieved to see the boy, though. He might not feel the same way when they caught up to their quarry, but right now it was different.

Eyes narrowed, he said, "You track me by moon?"

"By scent, like a blind hound dog."

Garner smiled in spite of himself. "You eat anything?"

"Jerky in the saddle," Hobie replied. He began to strip the tack off his horse.

"Fly's holding up nice," Garner remarked, casting an expert eye over the buckskin. Hobie always knew how to take care of a horse. It had to be born into you, Garner figured. Some men just came that way, and some others never got it.

"Yessir, he sure is," Hobie said with a grin. He patted the horse's neck. "He's a good 'un."

"Well, get him settled in and fed," Garner said, reaching for the coffeepot. "I'll slap some chuck together for you."

Hobie hesitated. "Boss?"

Garner looked up from the coffeepot, one brow arched. "What? You don't figure I can be trusted with Arbuckle's and a hunk of cold, smoked pronghorn?"

All of a sudden, Hobie broke out in a grin. "That'd be just fine, Boss," he said.

Garner drank a cup of coffee while Hobie ate and told him about his travels with Trevor and Woolsey, and he snorted when Hobie came to the part about the lawsuit-crazy bartender and High Draw, and especially Trevor and the spellbound crowd.

"Damn jackass," Garner muttered. "But that's the Marshals Service for you. Bunch of showboaters. You know, I sort of liked Marcus Trevor. Never rode with him before, but he's a personable cuss, and I'd heard good things about him from Holling Eberhart. Guess he was misled." Garner shook his head. "Those federal boys are all sizzle and no steak."

Squint-eyed, Hobie paused, his cup inches from his lips. "Every one'a them?"

Garner backed off just a tad. "Well, not *every* one, exactly. Most, though. It's a political job." He began to roll himself a smoke. "They've got their good ones here and there. A few of 'em are awful good. You pass that place where one of 'em got shot?"

"The U.S. marshals?" Hobie asked, his brows knitted. And then he grinned a little foolishly and said, "Oh, sorry. Yeah, I did. What you figure happened?"

Garner smoked and said his piece, and Hobie looked pretty darned relieved.

"Don't go gettin' all relaxed, kid," Garner cautioned. "They're both still out there." He stubbed out his cigarette.

"Yeah, but accordin' to you, there's likely to be one less by mornin'," Hobie said, and stuffed the last dry, stringy piece of smoked pronghorn into his mouth. "That's somethin' I can live with," he said around it.

"Me, too," said Garner, and tossed his remaining coffee out into the brush. He heard it hit with a faint splat. "You'd best get some sleep. I want to cut out of here first thing in the morning."

Hobie said, "Yessir, Boss," as Garner lay down and settled his hat over his eyes.

Despite everything, it surely did feel good to have the boy there with him.

Beneath his hat, he snorted at himself. Now, exactly when had he gotten so old that he welcomed the company of a young pup like Hobie?

•   •   •

Quietly, carefully, and with a certain amount of pain from his injury, Donny Belasco crept down toward the ruined house and its sleeping occupant. He led his horse, whose hooves he had padded with his extra clothing so that they made no sound.

He left the horse on the far side of the structure, tethered to a bush, then made his way silently around to the melted-down wall. Martindale's steady snores were the only sounds in the night.

Belasco slipped over the wall, careful to make no sound. Martindale kept on snoring. He crouched at Martindale's feet, studying him in the moonlight as the man blissfully sawed wood. This had been easier than he had imagined.

And Martindale looked so peaceful.

Belasco drew his side arm, flipped it around in his hand, than hammered the worn sole of Martindale's boot with its butt.

Martindale immediately pulled himself into a groggy sit, muttering, "What? What?"

And then he saw Belasco, and his expression changed immediately from one of sleepy curiosity to dread.

"Y-you," was all he said. He eyed Belasco's gun, which was leveled at him.

Belasco smiled. "Hello, old *amigo*. Old buddy. Old pal."

"Y-you mad about . . . back there?" Martindale asked. His voice was breathy and low. "'Bout that little, um, accident?"

"Now, what do you think, Vincent?"

Martindale seemed to mull it over. He swallowed hard, and in a thick, strangled voice asked, "Why ain't you dead?"

"Because unlike you, my darling, I plan ahead," Belasco answered, and rapped, with a dull metallic sound, on his stomach.

Martindale's features bunched up.

Belasco rolled his eyes, then pulled out his shirttail, exposing the metal sign. "Armor, you idiotic twit," he said.

Martindale swallowed again. "You gonna kill me?"

"Oh, yes indeed, Vincent, yes indeed," Belasco said, never rising from his squat. He tucked his shirt back in, and his smile broadened. "Eventually." He reached into his pocket and pulled out a length of cord, then tossed it to Martindale.

Martindale stared at it. "What?"

Belasco shook his head and clicked his tongue. "Now, Vincent, really. Tie yourself up, dear boy, and be quick about it. Don't go near that gun of yours, or I shall be forced to shoot you in the arm. In fact, toss it over there. Two fingers. Easy, now."

Martindale wasn't any too quick about anything, however. But he tossed the pistol about three feet away, tied his boots upon Belasco's instructions, and then his left wrist.

"Now what?" he asked.

"Over on your belly," Belasco said, wiggling the gun's nose. "Hands behind your back."

"No," Martindale said mulishly.

Belasco's brows went up. "I beg your pardon, Vincent? Did I just hear you say no?"

Martindale scowled. "Shoot me. Just shoot me right here. I seen what you done to those women. I ain't gonna let you near me with that razor, so just go ahead and do it right now."

Belasco hadn't expected this, precisely. A valiant

struggle before the ropes went on perhaps, or a latent re-alization, one final look of horror as he began to slice. But he hadn't counted on Martindale's pulling on the brakes when he was halfway trussed. Why, it didn't make any sense!

Of course, nothing Martindale did had the slightest bit of sense to it, did it?

"So you're in character after all," Belasco said softly.

Martindale's features bunched. "Huh?"

Belasco stood up. He wiggled his gun. "Turn over. Now."

"Nope," said Martindale firmly, and crossed his arms. "Ain't gonna do it."

Martindale had Belasco at something of a disadvantage. Even roped and halfway trussed, he was certainly the stronger of the two of them, and Belasco chided himself for not taking this possibility into consideration.

"All right," he said at last. "Stand up."

"I can't," Martindale said petulantly. "Not with my feet tied."

"I'll assist you, then," said Belasco.

Martindale scowled, but before he could say, "What?" Belasco added, "I'll help you to your feet."

"Oh," said Martindale. He leaned forward and slung his tightly secured boots to one side, then hesitated, hands outstretched and propping him up. "What you gonna do then, Belasco?" he said with just a hint of a smile.

Belasco saw him push himself to the side and reach his discarded side arm, saw it slither into his grasp, saw it arcing up.

And he kicked Martindale in the side of the head just as hard as he could.

The gun flew across the small dwelling so hard and fast that when it hit the wall, adobe chips sprayed out in a fan. Martindale lay unconscious on the floor.

"Donny, Donny, Donny," Belasco chided himself as he quickly tied Martindale's hands behind his back. "Next time, think things through, for heaven's sake!"

He rolled Martindale back over, took a moment to catch his breath and wipe his brow, then pulled two bandannas from another pocket. One, he rolled into a wad and stuffed into Martindale's mouth. The second, he tied over it and around Martindale's head. And then he unbuttoned Martindale's trousers and yanked them down to his knees.

He found Martindale's canteen and splashed the man's face with water.

Martindale came to with a half-strangled sputter and gave a hard snort that dirtied his gag with thick mucus. "Mmm!" he tried to shout in protest. "Mmm! Mmm!" More bubbles came from his nose.

"Now, now, Vincent," Belasco said calmly. "No use fighting it." He reached into a final pocket and brought out his razor. He opened it. The blade glinted in the moonlight.

Martindale's eye grew wide and fairly bugged from their sockets. He tried to speak again, or perhaps beg—that was more likely, Belasco thought matter-of-factly—and frantically shook his head over and over in a silent "no-no-no."

Brightly, Belasco said, "Let's get started, shall we?" and sat, dropping all of his weight on Martindale's midsection and knocking the air out of his lungs with a *whoosh.*

Martindale got his air back and erupted into a high, muffled squeal at the same moment that Belasco showed him the first ear, glistening red and dripping. It was large and filthy and a little hairy, but it was an ear nonetheless.

Lips pursed, Belasco laid it carefully on Martindale's chest.

Thoughtfully, he said, "You know, Vincent, I was worried that this might be a tad distasteful, you being of the male persuasion and all. But in actuality, I'm finding it quite enjoyable."

Humming, Belasco bent back to his work.

Martindale began to scream anew.

15

At about nine o'clock the next morning, Garner and Hobie rode up to the top of a gentle slope and stopped while Garner got down and had himself a good look at the ground.

"Stopped for a while, didn't he?" Hobie asked, his eyes toward the ground. There were lots of scuff marks and hoofprints where a horse had stood, and a long, bent-down place where a man had stretched out for a good bit. Hobie was having a little trouble with the scuff marks, though, and gave his ear a rub.

"Yeah, and he wrapped his horse's hooves," Garner said, answering Hobie's unspoken question. He stood up with his back to Hobie and faced the old hovel down the hill. "It was Belasco," he said with conviction. "Martindale never would have thought to bide his time, let alone pad out his horse."

Grimly, he turned toward Hobie. "I reckon we're

gonna find something nasty down the hill." He stuck his foot in the stirrup.

"Yessir," Hobie said as Garner swung into the saddle. "I figured as much."

Hobie dreaded what he guessed they were about to discover, but it didn't stop him from doggedly following Garner down the gentle slope, toward the ruined building. The roof was all burnt off, he noted, although that had probably happened decades ago by the crumbly look of the walls. He couldn't see much inside it even though one of the walls was half gone. He found himself hoping that Martindale had dragged Belasco off somewhere, or vice versa.

He didn't much care who had killed whom, just so long as one of them was dead. It would make one less for them to track, and frankly, now that the reality of finding yet another body was before him, Hobie was thinking that he'd had about enough of this hero business. Garner seemed fair determined, though, like he had something driving him that Hobie couldn't begin to understand, not really. All Hobie wanted to do was catch this fellow, whichever one was left over, and get back up home. Start putting up canned goods again and halter-breaking foals. Get back to a normal life.

Garner pulled up Faro and tied him to a bush, had a quick glance at the ground, then rounded the house. Hobie tied Fly, too, but he took his time following Garner. He stared at the ground. The horse with the padded hooves had stood here for quite some time before somebody unwrapped him and rode him off. There was no sign of the other outlaw's mount, at least, not here. Maybe the second one had grabbed him farther out and taken him along.

Or maybe Martindale and Belasco had made up and

ridden off together. That would be good, because he wouldn't have to look at the results of one murdering the other. But bad, because there'd still be the two of them out there, somewhere.

"Hobie!" Garner shouted.

Hobie gave his head a quick shake and followed Garner's path at a trot.

He found Garner inside the shell of the house, standing over what was left of a body, and the first thing Hobie did was to turn around and lose his breakfast, right there in the dirt-floored house.

He had never seen such a thing, never imagined such a thing, in his whole life. He'd been told, of course, been told about the evil things Belasco did to people, but seeing it was different.

"You all right, boy?" Garner asked, not unkindly.

Hobie threw up again.

Garner stood there while Hobie continued to be sick behind him, and he stared at what was left of Martindale. He'd been bound with his hands behind his back and his feet tied. The still-sodden rag at his side attested to the fact that he'd been gagged, so that he was denied even the comfort of a good, loud scream.

His ears had been cut off, and his nose and eyelids. All while he was still alive, Garner was fairly certain. Plenty of blood. But if that wasn't bad enough, what Belasco had done next was enough to turn Garner's stomach.

Belasco had broken his pattern in more ways than one. He hadn't slit Martindale's throat. Martindale's britches were pulled down to his knees, and his penis and testicles had been cut off and inserted in his mouth.

Unconsciously, Garner touched himself, just to make sure he was still all there.

He'd seen this before, but only when the perpetrators were Apache, and only once and long ago. Martindale had most certainly been alive for the de-sexing. In fact, he'd likely bled to death from it. Below the gaping wound in his groin, the ground was soaked dark red and buzzing with flies. A few more days, and Martindale would only have maggots where his pecker used to be.

"Hobie?" Garner said again, and tried to keep himself from choking. Somebody had to hold himself together, for God's sake.

He got a weak "Yeah, Boss" in reply.

"Sorry, Hobie," he said. "Get back on your horse."

This time there was no answer, just the sound of scuffing feet as the boy climbed over the wall and went back toward the horses.

"Poor sonofabitch," Garner muttered, although it wasn't clear whether the sentiment was for Martindale or Hobie. He didn't know himself, although he kept on telling himself that he shouldn't feel the slightest concern for Martindale. Somebody who threw live people into burning buildings wasn't deserving of any sympathy whatsoever.

But the way he'd died . . .

Abruptly, Garner turned on his heel and followed Hobie to the horses. "Sorry I hollered for you," he said gruffly as he mounted up. "I changed my mind. We're not gonna take the time to bury the sonofabitch."

Hobie looked white as milk. He also didn't look even slightly disappointed that they weren't going to hang around and hold services. "Fine with me," he whispered just loud enough for Garner to hear.

Garner reined Faro away, and Hobie followed.

"Got the trail?" Garner asked.

Hobie nodded.

"Fine. Then you lead for a while."

Hobie, still pale, wiped at his mouth. Garner knew just how he felt.

Hobie didn't answer him, just nodded weakly and jogged out in front.

Up ahead, Belasco had just changed horses and was loping along on Martindale's mount.

He had thought about shooting his own exhausted mount, thinking it would be too easily seen out here on this flat desert land, but then decided that a shot would be noisy indeed, and he couldn't be certain how close he was being followed. Or if he was being followed at all, for that matter.

In the end, he'd simply cut the horse's throat. It had made quite a lovely gush of blood as it stood there, questioning him with its soft brown eyes. Then it had fallen to its knees, into the brush, and groaned its last.

Right at the moment, however, he was wondering if he should have let the beast live. Martindale's mud-brown horse was by far the inferior of the two, being not in the smallest part nimble-footed. It tripped over its own hooves roughly every fifteen seconds, and had nearly pitched him off twice because of its clumsiness.

Ah, well, he thought cockily. He'd purchase a decent mount in the first town he came to. Which, according to his calculations, should be Half Moon Crossing. Then he'd take the ferry across the Colorado and lose himself in California for a bit. Maybe he'd ramble on up to San Francisco again. He hadn't been there for eons. It was easy for a man to get lost in San Francisco, as he remembered.

On second thought, perhaps he'd hie himself down south of the border for a while, really throw those stupid dogs of the law off his trail.

He was certain they had quite a few pretty soiled doves in Mexico, too.

"Oh, Mother Dearest," he whispered into the wind beating at his face, "if you could see what your little boy has grown up to be."

He grinned.

"Excuse me," Woolsey asked, "but can't we make better time? We seem to be going terribly slow." He didn't add that he felt like a very small tortoise chasing a very large hare.

Woolsey had been thinking that he should have ridden off with that twit, Hobie, instead of staying with the deputy. In fact, he was certain of it. At least he'd be seeing something besides the south end of a northbound gray horse.

"Not if you want to stay on the damn trail," Deputy Trevor growled.

Touchy, Woolsey thought in irritation. Very touchy. You bastard.

In all fairness, though, he supposed this must be highly embarrassing for Trevor. After all, the man had purported his skills to be past superhuman in all areas. Woolsey had known this was hyperbole, but he hadn't counted on the extent of it. Why, without Garner or Hobie to track for him, Trevor was as good as lost, and Woolsey with him.

Perfect, he thought bitterly as he watched Trevor's long sandy curls—now filthy and oily and dark with dirt from the trail—swinging to and fro over the man's back. How perfect. Lost in the wilds of Arizona with ten pounds of hair on a horse.

And this mule he was forced to ride! Charlie Blue had so far tried to take extremely large bites out of assorted parts of his body, and had nearly succeeded twice. Woolsey had great, massive, purple bruises on his arm and back, he just knew it. They were certainly as sore as Hades.

Besides which, he was sure that he had calluses on his calluses, in places where a cultivated man shouldn't have calluses at all.

He'd vowed long ago that he'd get into no more drinking bets with colleagues, and now he vowed that as soon as this idiot of a deputy marshal got him back to some semblance of civilization, he would never, ever, so much as put his foot near a stirrup again.

And he would shoot on sight any mule that crossed his path. No questions asked.

"Okay," said Trevor somewhat grudgingly, and reined in his horse. Woolsey nearly ran into the gray's back end, and stopped Charlie Blue just in time.

"Yes?" he replied, turning the mule slightly to one side before he could take a bite out of Trevor's gray. "What?"

Trevor pointed out across the plain that Woolsey had just realized was there ahead of them. They'd been going through rocks and up and down hills for as long as he could remember, it seemed. And through the broad, brushy plain, he could just make out a path.

He squinted. The path grew more distinct, like a loose braid drawn in trampled spring grasses and treaded-upon wildflowers.

"Well, my goodness," he said.

"And you said I didn't know what I was doin'," Trevor sneered.

"I never any such thing," Woolsey said. "I merely questioned your tactics."

"Yeah, sure," Trevor grumbled, and reined his horse down the last hill, toward the plain.

Woolsey gave the mule a kick and followed.

When they got down on the flat, Trevor set out in a dead gallop and Charlie Blue followed, much to Woolsey's despair. It was hard enough to cling to this dreadful beast at a jarring trot, much less a dead run. He gave up all hope of steering the animal with his reins, and simply threw his arms around the mule's neck, closed his windburnt eyes, and hung on for dear life.

After what seemed an age of being nearly jounced from the saddle, nearly tossed into the thorny cactus and left for dead, the mule slowed and Woolsey cracked open one eye.

Ahead, Trevor had stopped and dismounted. He was kicking at something.

"What did you find?" Woolsey shouted, his fists still full of Charlie Blue's mane.

"They camped," Trevor called back. "Two of 'em."

The mule jogged up roughly even with Trevor's gray and stopped, and Woolsey gratefully slid to the ground. Bent over, hands on his knees, he said, "Which two, Deputy?"

Trevor was silent, and Woolsey looked up to see him walking out into the brush and back again, kneeling every few steps. Then, theatrically, he stopped and pointed ahead. "Garner and Hobie," he said in a booming voice. "Their tracks are on top of the first pair of horses."

Well, my goodness, thought Woolsey disdainfully. Don't *we* have our confidence back!

"I figure they camped here for the night," Trevor went on, bravado oozing from his every pore. "Yes, indeed. They camped and ate . . ." He bent to the ground, picked something up, something tiny he found beside the remains of the fire, and tested it thoughtfully between his teeth.

"Pronghorn jerky," he announced assuredly. "The selfsame stuff I brung from Tucson. Yessirree Bob." Then, scowling, he turned to face Woolsey square on. "How's that for trackin', Mr. Highfalutin Newspaper Reporter? Why don't you write that down?"

Woolsey stood up slowly, feeling every muscle in his back and haunches complain. "Excellent, Deputy Trevor, excellent," he said without much enthusiasm. "I most certainly will."

Not on your tintype, he added mentally. They had passed signs of some sort of scuffle a few minutes back. Anyone could see it, even a squinting man riding a mule at a full gallop. After all, he had noticed the bent-down grass and weeds, seen the dark places on the ground that he assumed were dried blood, and seen the signs of two more horses passing over it.

But not this highfalutin peacock of a deputy. Woolsey had long since given up any hope of getting a decent story out of the chase, not with Garner so far away.

He'd certainly misjudged Garner. At least the man seem to be well ahead of them—and Hobie was too—and hot on these villains' trail. All the excitement of the arrests would be theirs, and he would miss it entirely.

It wasn't fair.

Oh, he could write about the chase, but what was a good chase without a climax? Nothing, if you asked him. Most probably that was what his editor would answer, too.

Woolsey had staked his money on the wrong horse, and he knew it.

However, he considered that it would do well for him to keep in Trevor's good graces for the time being. He most assuredly did not wish to end up deserted in the stark middle of nowhere.

The mule, who had so far behaved himself, chose that moment to clamp his teeth down on Woolsey's thigh, and Woolsey let out a painful yelp.

"Let me go!" he cried, beating his fists ineffectually against the mule's thick skull. "Let go, you son of Satan!"

Charlie Blue gave him the evil eye and surrendered his leg, but only because Deputy Trevor had taken hold of his reins and jerked his head away. For a moment, Woolsey thought a good portion of his thigh was going to go with him.

Trevor stood there, holding the reins and grinning. "Hurt much?" he asked, pushing his hat back.

Woolsey rubbed his leg, smearing the mule's spit all over his pants. "Please," Woolsey said, staring at his damp hands in distaste. "Could you refrain from belittling my pain for just a few minutes?"

And then he felt fury practically leaping from his pores. "My pants!" he cried. "This smelly, flea-ridden son of a donkey has ripped my trousers!"

Trevor peered closer and tilted his head. "Ain't much," he said. "Most folks wouldn't hardly notice it a'tall."

Woolsey snatched his reins from Trevor's grasp and fairly leapt up on Charlie Blue. He took firm hold of the beast's mouth and backed him up.

"Says you," Woolsey spat, and reined the mule away, belatedly realizing that he'd just stooped to Trevor's level. Make a snide remark, then ride away, that was the pattern, wasn't it?

He put a hand to his forehead and rubbed hard. I don't suppose, he thought, that I could get into the good graces of a back-East paper with a rousing story on needlepoint. . . .

The sooner he got back to civilization, the better.

16

"Goddamn it!" Garner spat.

He stood in the late afternoon sun, staring down at the dead horse and the buzzards that perched on its saddle, squawking and arguing. There wasn't a blessed thing wrong with it. No legs busted, no tendons bowed. No, Belasco had killed it because it was tired, that was all, and would slow him down. And probably because he didn't want it sticking out on the plain if he simply left it behind. And also because he was too damn lazy to strip its tack off and spook it off his trail.

He'd forgotten about the buzzards, though. They'd probably been on this poor horse within a half hour or less. Course, by then, Belasco would have been long gone. He wouldn't have noticed, riding hell-bent for leather like he was.

This horse made Garner madder than Martindale's murder and mutilation. Sure, there was no rhyme or reason to that, either, but at least you had to figure that

Martindale sort of deserved it. But this horse hadn't deserved any such thing.

At least Belasco wasn't inclined to practice his more grisly hobbies on the animal kingdom. One clean slice to the jugular, it looked like.

Didn't make Garner any less angry, though.

"Boss?" Hobie said quietly from behind him. "What you wanna do?"

"Nothin', I guess," he answered after a moment's silence, then suddenly turned back toward the dead horse and ran at it, shouting and flapping his arms.

The buzzards rose up and hopped off in angry black clouds, and Garner resolutely stepped back up on Faro, but not before he gave him a pat on the neck. "Too late to do anything but ride the sonofabitch down," he said.

"We're gonna have to be awful quick about it," Hobie said.

"He's down to the one horse now," Garner said, pushing Faro into a ground-eating jog before he had to watch the buzzards come back in for their feed. "He's gonna have to slow up. We won't catch him today, that's for sure, but tomorrow's another matter."

"What if he crosses the river?" Hobie asked. He looked a whole lot better than he had this morning when they'd found Martindale, but he'd still been kind of sick at noon and turned down lunch. "Goes into California, I mean."

Garner looked over at him. "You got anything against California, Hobie?"

"No, but . . ."

"We just keep on following him, that's all," Garner said. "Unless you want to go back home. You can leave anytime. No grudges held."

For a moment, he was positive that Hobie was going

to tip his hat and wish him luck, and Garner figured he couldn't blame him. But Hobie said, "Nope, Boss. I reckon I'm in till the end."

Garner wanted to say something like, "I'm glad to have you along, Hobie," or, "I'm proud of you, son," or even, "You'd best eat your supper tonight, Hobie, get something in your belly." But Garner being Garner, he said none of those things. He just grunted noncommittally and urged Faro into a lope.

Hobie followed.

They camped in a hollow at the onset of a small range of hills, little more than gravelly, brushy bumps in the ground, really. They had ridden the horses as hard as they'd dared, and Garner took special care to rub down Faro and make him comfortable. Hobie did the same with Fly, he noticed. Good boy.

They made a fire and started coffee to boiling and beans to soaking. Garner figured to be pretty close to Belasco now. The tracks they'd followed after they discovered Belasco's murdered horse had been sloppy, made by a horse that toed in and fell over its own feet half the time. For not the first time since they started after these boys, Garner wondered that the damn nag didn't fall down and kill itself.

Belasco had surely killed the wrong horse, that was for certain. This one was slower-paced, and by the looks of the trail Belasco was down to a jog, period, within an hour of switching horses.

Caught your own tit in the wringer this time, didn't you, you crazy sonofabitch, Garner thought as he stirred the beans. He wouldn't have a moment's grief over gunning down that mad dog. Too bad he didn't have the nerve to cut him up some first. Belasco had it coming.

"Cloudy," Hobie said when he came and sat across

the fire. The sky had, indeed, gone spotty and gray, and the dying sun barely peeked through the clouds. "Gonna be good and dark tonight, by the looks of it," he said.

Garner handed him a cup of coffee. "Yeah, unless the moon burns 'em off."

Hobie managed a smile. "Yeah, sure," he said. He took a drink of coffee.

It wasn't boiled as strong as Garner liked it, but he figured Hobie'd best take it a little weak right at first. No telling what shape his gullet was in.

"You know what I can't figure?" Hobie said over his cup. "I can't figure how if Belasco got wounded back there where we saw the blood, he could take out Martindale."

Garner shrugged. "Maybe it was Martindale that got wounded."

Hobie made a face. "From everything you fellers have been talkin' about, Donny Belasco wouldn't just leave Martindale there hurt. He'd make sure he was killed all the way."

Garner nodded. "Got a point, Hobie."

The boy seemed to perk up some.

"Maybe it was just a flesh wound," Garner said, and pulled out the fixings for biscuits.

"Um, Boss?" said Hobie, lifting a brow.

"Yeah, good idea," Garner said, and tossed ingredients, one by one, across the fire to Hobie. "Leastwise, it was something that looked serious enough that Martindale took off, figuring he was free as a bird. Scalp wound maybe," he added, and began rolling himself a smoke. "They bleed a lot even when they're not serious."

"Boss?" Hobie had paused with his batter in mid-stir.

"Yeah?"

"When this is all over and we go up home again, let's just stay there, all right?"

Garner gave the cigarette a last lick and flicked a sulphur tip into flame. Holding it to his smoke, he said, "You got yourself a deal, Hobie."

Belasco had been readying to slip down to the ranch at nightfall. It wasn't much. A tiny house, a couple of sheds, and a lean-to that had hopes of becoming a barn someday. That, and two people. A mother and grown daughter, by the looks of it. No telling where the menfolk were, but at least they weren't here.

He had decided to wait until after dark to go in. First of all, he wanted to make sure their men weren't going to come home all of a sudden. Second, he figured that he'd look more pitiful at night.

Thank God I found this place, ma'am. I'm terrible lost. Can you help a poor boy?

He grinned hungrily.

Belasco took a look another look through his spyglass. They'd gone inside, lit the lamps. The glow washed gold out the tiny windows. A silhouette passed, blocking the light momentarily, then passed on. The older one, he thought. They were both of an age, though, slender and full-busted. The younger one was blond and quite pretty.

He stood up and walked back toward where he'd secreted the mud-brown horse. A piece of garbage, that's what it was. Those women had a decent saddle horse, a pinto, under the lean-to. He figured to take it once he'd finished with them.

It would be his last job before he ferried across the river into California.

He had just mounted his horse when he chanced to swing his head down toward the south. Something glinted and winked, something tiny, and he paused. He squinted and stared. This wasn't good, wasn't good at all. He pulled out the spyglass again and raised it to his eye.

He snorted in disgust. The glow of a campfire, he was sure of it: very distant, probably less than an hour's ride behind him, but it was there, all right, and who in their right mind would be out here unless he was chasing somebody—or being chased? He collapsed the spyglass with more force than necessary.

Damn and blast!

Belasco was faced with a choice. He could just go on the way he'd been going, skinny over into California and try to lose himself. He'd come nearly to Half Moon Crossing, nearly to the river.

His pursuer would have to figure that California was where he was heading, wouldn't he?

He scowled, and stepped down off the horse again.

All right. Two could play at this game.

Belasco sat down again. He'd wait. He'd give those two biddies time to go to sleep, then he'd slip down and take their horse. It couldn't be worse than this one. And then he'd double back, swinging out to the east. He'd head south again, generally speaking, and go into Mexico. He spoke a smattering of Spanish, enough to get along. And just give him a couple of weeks. Why, he'd be speaking it like a native.

He leaned back, and the smile, that deceptively ingenuous boy's smile, returned to his face. "Here I come, lovely *señoritas*," he whispered into the darkness. "A little sooner than anticipated, but here I come nonetheless."

• • •

Beside the dying campfire, King Garner woke with a start. He'd been dreaming of poor Annie Cartwell and those that had come before her, and he was glad something had woken him.

He held himself still, not breathing, listening.

There it was. Just faintly. The sound of distant, galloping hooves, coming from the northwest, heading toward the southeast.

He waited a moment before he gave the alarm, though. Out here, canyons and juts of land could play tricks on the ears. Except he didn't figure there were many canyons up that way, or juts of land, either.

The hoofbeats faded, and he hissed, "Hobie!"

The boy mumbled something in his sleep and turned over.

"Damn it, wake up!" Garner struggled to his feet. His left leg didn't want to wake up, and he began to stomp his boot on the ground. "Get up or I'll shoot you, Hobie," he growled.

"What?" Hobie grumbled, and rubbed at his eyes. "Is it five yet?"

"No, it's about half past one, but you'd better get up if you want to catch Belasco." Garner swept up his bedroll and started limping toward the horses. Damn leg. He must have slept on it crooked, because now it felt like it was full of bicarbonate of soda.

Hobie leapt to his feet, something Garner wished he still had the ability to do. "Why? What? Where is he?" Hobie's head twisted like an owl's.

Garner threw the saddle up on Faro. "Headed southeast. Dammit, if I'd been thinking straight, I would've known better than to build that fire."

But Hobie simply stood there, legs on either side of

his bedding. "Boss? Did you see him? And if you did, how come one of you ain't dead?"

Garner reached for the girth strap. "I heard him. And hurry the hell up. He's turned back and heading for the border."

"But how do you figure it was him?" Hobie insisted. "Did you see him? What'd he do, ride by and holler at you?"

Garner gave a final tug to the strap and reached for Faro's bridle. "Fine," he said, dead serious. "You just stay here and plod after his track come morning. I'm goin' after him now."

"But there ain't no moon!" Hobie cried. "It's clouded over, remember?"

Garner hiked a thumb heavenward. "Not anymore."

Hobie looked up to see a sky nearly clear of clouds. The moon was full no longer, but it still put out a good deal of light. "Aw, turds," he grumbled.

Garner stepped up on Faro. "Follow me if you want to, kid," he said. "Your choice."

He cantered out into the night.

Hobie stood there a good long time, wondering what the heck to do. Belasco was up ahead of them, he was sure of it, but now Garner was heading southeast. If Garner had heard something, he couldn't be sure it was Belasco, could he?

Maybe this lust Garner had for catching Belasco had invaded his dreams to the extent that he thought he'd heard him, big as life.

Except that Garner had about as much imagination as a tree stump. He wouldn't have made it up. Wouldn't even have crossed his mind to do so.

With a sigh, Hobie scooped up his bedding. If Belasco was up ahead—where Hobie truly thought he was—there was no way on this green earth that he was going to go up there all by his lonesome and try to bring him in. He'd end up like Martindale if he tried that.

He gave an involuntary shudder, then stood up a little straighter.

No, sir. He wasn't going to go to Jesus all cut up like that. He'd stick with King Garner for better or worse. If it turned out to be a fool's errand, well, they'd just have to add a week or so onto the time it would take to catch Belasco and head for home.

He headed for Fly. If he was going to catch up with Garner, he'd have to hurry.

17

Belasco was heading south, and in a considerable hurry. He'd gone too close to where that man—or those men—were camped. He hadn't realized it until it was nearly too late, but how was he to suspect that they'd let their fire go so low that a body couldn't see it from a distance?

Thank God there was some moon, and thank God that this newest nag was halfway nimble-footed. He had stolen it with no problem whatsoever, and left Martindale's walking dog meat in its place. He'd also kept his distance from the house. The ladies of the little ranch hadn't known how close they came to the pleasure of his company.

But now, this fiasco! He only hoped that the camp hadn't had someone sitting up on guard duty, someone who would have heard him passing. That would be just the frosting on the cake, wouldn't it?

The horse, a plain-headed pinto mare, was tiring beneath him, and he grudgingly slowed her to a jog.

"Fifteen minutes, my dear," he said under his breath. "Fifteen minutes, and then you gallop again. I trust you understand me."

The horse wearily jogged on.

About a half mile from where Garner and Hobie had camped, Garner was slowly working Faro back and forth, looking for signs, Hobie was some distance out to his left, doing the same.

Everything was different at night. The soft spring weeds turned silver, and their shadows and the gravel seemed to hide tracks that should have shown plain.

"Goddamn it," Garner muttered for the fourth or fifth time. Had he really made it up after all? Was old age setting in so bad that he couldn't even trust his ears anymore?

And then Hobie hollered, "Here!" and waved an arm.

Relieved, Garner trotted up to him.

Hobie pointed at the ground. "Came through here sure as shootin', Boss. In some kind of a hurry, too." The kid was grinning with excitement, and the tracks were plain. Or as plain as they could be at night with just that old moon up there.

"Good job, kid," Garner said before he realized it.

Hobie looked ready to bust all his buttons.

"Aw, don't get carried away with yourself," Garner grumbled. "We haven't caught him yet."

Hobie kept on smiling, though.

They followed the track at a walk, a jog if Garner felt comfortable about it and the trail was plain. Belasco may not care if he rides his horse into a hole and kills it, he thought, but I do.

"Hey, Boss?" Hobie asked after about a half hour. "How'd you know it was Belasco?"

"I don't," Garner replied. "Not for certain."

"Then why—"

"Because I got a feelin', that's why," Garner interrupted. He opened his canteen and took a long drink. "You do this kind of thing for a few years, you get to trust your feelings."

"Excuse me for sayin' it," Hobie went on, "but what if your feelin's wrong? Not that I want to turn around or anything."

Garner stoppered his canteen. "Then I'm too damned old for this crud, after all."

Garner hadn't realized that he'd snapped, but Hobie said, "You don't need to go gettin' all mad. I was just askin'."

"Not mad at you, kid. I'm mad at the whole damn situation." Garner followed the track in a wide swerve around a clump of jumping cholla. "I'm mad at Marcus Trevor for trickin' me into it, mad at Holling Eberhart for givin' him a job in the first place. I'm mad at the jokers who let Donny Belasco jump prison, but mostly I'm mad at me, because I didn't kill the baby-faced sonofabitch all those years ago when I had a chance."

There was a pause, and then Hobie said, "Oh."

He remained silent for quite some time, and Garner didn't say anything, either. He just followed the trail.

Belasco was making excellent time.

He had rejoined his own track about a half hour ago and came to—and passed—the ruined house where he'd left Martindale. He didn't look inside. He didn't have to. When he killed somebody, they were most finally, assuredly dead.

His horse was becoming wearier and wearier, and he

was having to walk more often than not. Irritating, but necessary.

He planned to retrace his trail from here on out, perhaps until he got down around Slewfoot. Slewfoot was still there, wasn't it? A little gnat of a town, no more important and perhaps less busy than High Draw had been. Well, no matter. He'd bypassed it before, but this time he'd leave the trail and cut through Slewfoot, then straight south to Mexico.

He only wished he had another mount right here and now. He wouldn't be so stupid as he'd been before. He wouldn't kill this horse. No, he'd just vault onto the second horse and lead this one until the second one gave out, then switch again. That made a great deal more sense.

Over the gentle hills he rode, sometimes at a walk, sometimes at a soft jog. Sometimes, when the horse appeared a little less tired, at a slow lope. The night was bright, he was certain he'd outpaced his pursuers, and he had a clear line to Mexico. What more could a man ask for?

As he cantered along, the horse beneath him suddenly jolted to the right, then went head over heels, throwing him clear.

He landed on his hip, and it was a second before the pain cleared enough that he heard the horse moaning, heard it struggling to stand.

Slowly, carefully, he stood up and limped to the fallen horse. Even in the moonlight he could see that both the front legs were broken, the bone poking at a sharp angle from one, and every futile attempt the mare made to put weight on her legs caused the breaks to worsen. Her eyes were ringed with white, and lather from her body coated the bushes.

"You bitch," said Belasco, his voice flat. "You stupid bitch."

With great difficulty, he knelt down and freed his saddlebags and canteens, then took the razor from his pocket.

"You sorry excuse for a horse," he muttered.

An hour later, Belasco was on foot, saddlebags over his shoulder, walking through the dark across the vast open plain he'd crossed the day before. He had to admit that he'd made excellent time up until the damned horse had gone and stepped in a hole. He'd more than erased his last day's travel and then some.

But if he didn't find himself some transportation pretty soon, he was going to be up the creek without the proverbial paddle.

Whatever he'd hurt in his hip when the blasted nag threw him had stopped hurting so sharply. He was certain that once he stopped and slept for a couple of hours it would come back to haunt him, but for the moment, it was something he could stand.

He paused to dip into his pocket for his timepiece, and flipped the case open. He turned it so that the moon shone on the dial.

A little after four. He supposed he should find a place to hide fairly soon. Within the next hour and a half, anyway. The sun would be coming up before six, and he didn't want to be afoot out here when it did.

But any shelter seemed impossibly far away. The hills edging the desert were miles and miles away, he knew, despite the fact that he could make out their rambling bulk quite plainly. They looked like a line of deep purple . . . What was that stuff that women sewed on clothing as decoration? Ah, yes. Rickrack. They looked like a line of dark rickrack, sewn to a crooked horizon.

There would be no shelter for him there, not at this snail's pace.

And then, miracle of miracles, he thought he saw a light.

It wasn't very bright. Just a little flicker—now there, now gone, now there again—up ahead.

But he hadn't been wrong. Somebody was camped up ahead. Somebody whose fire was still going, just barely. It couldn't be a party of marshals, could it? No, he'd passed them earlier. They were probably still snoring beside their stupid fire.

He supposed it could be reinforcements. Then again, perhaps not. Perhaps just some pilgrim or a saddle tramp.

He sighed. Well, my goodness. Whoever it was would have to have horses, wouldn't they?

Just one was all he needed.

He switched the heavy saddlebags to his left shoulder, took a swig from his canteen, and set off with new resolve toward the distant campfire.

"I'm a-comin'," he sang softly. "I'm a-comin', though my head is hangin' low. . . ."

Woolsey dreamt of New York, of its cabs and bustling streets—and the smell of manure piling at its curbs. He dreamt of the theater and bright lights and the electricity that made them glow, of restaurants that had never even thought of placing a grisly item like prairie oysters on the menu, and of newspaper offices—real newspapers—that smelled of printer's ink and sweat and excitement.

And then something came through his dream, something that had no business in New York at all. A kind of a thrash, then a grunt, then a gurgle.

Still half asleep, he muttered something, felt his lips move, at least, and was just starting to open his eyes when a heavy weight fell upon his chest.

His eyes came open then, all right, and he found himself pinned to the ground by a strange man-boy, a grinning fool with something shiny in his hand.

A razor.

Oddly enough, the first thing he thought of was to seek the protection of his inept traveling companion. "Deputy!" he cried in a voice tight with fear. "Deputy Trevor!"

The man on his chest smiled and muttered, "So that's who he was." Then, in a louder voice, he said, "I'm afraid he's otherwise occupied, my dear."

Realization hit Woolsey like a bucket of ice water thrown into his face. "M-Mr. Donald Belasco?" he said, feeling the all blood drain from his face. "*The* Donny Belasco?"

"Perspicacious of you, I must say," answered Belasco. "And who might you be?" Suddenly, Belasco made a face and added, "Tut-tut, sir. Don't try to move. I have your arms pinned."

He did indeed. His knees cut into Woolsey's upper arms like two-by-fours.

"Excuse me," whispered Woolsey. "And allow me to introduce myself, sir," he began. "I am Clive Woolsey, representing the famous *Tucson Herald* newspaper, and hopefully every major newspaper in the land, via the wire service."

"And?" asked Belasco. His face really was quite engaging, Woolsey thought. He would have had drinks at the club with him anytime. He was the sort of fellow one would introduce to his sister, if he had one. Except for sitting on one's chest, he seemed quite lucid. Charmingly so, in fact.

Woolsey gathered his courage. "And I should like to write about you. I should like to make you famous. I am planning an entire series of articles."

Belasco tipped his head and rested the razor along his temple thoughtfully. There was blood on it. "Really," he said. "How interesting."

Was it Woolsey's imagination, or had Belasco eased up the pressure on his upper arms?

"Yes indeed," Woolsey said, nodding his head. He wasn't quite so afraid anymore, despite having noticed the blood. Trevor's blood, he realized, and swallowed. But this Belasco seemed an intelligent fellow, for a homicidal maniac. He could be reasoned with, possibly. Woolsey had the power to make him a household name all over the country, for heaven's sake!

He cleared his throat. "I have ridden all the way from Tucson on that horrid mule to get your story. My editor is quite rabid to have it." And then he wondered if he should have used the word "rabid."

Belasco shifted his weight a little, and Woolsey felt a sharp pain in his side. He grimaced.

"Sorry, old chum," Belasco said as if they were back East, standing on the sidewalk in front of the Bijou Theater in the middle of the day. "It would seem I've cracked your ribs."

Something about the way he said it caused a resurgence of Woolsey's panic. He said, "I'm completely unarmed, I promise you."

"That's why I didn't kill you first," came the answer, cloaked by a sweet grin.

"Oh," said Woolsey. It was getting harder and harder

to breathe. "Oh, I see." And see, he did. The full realization of Deputy Trevor's murder was, well, sitting on
his chest.

"W-would you mind if I got up?" he asked, hoping
against hope. "I'll need my notepad."

"Oh, I don't believe you will," said Belasco, smiling.

18

Garner and Hobie, who had been holding to a much slower pace than their quarry, came upon the dead pinto at daybreak, when the sky was painted pink and crimson.

"Goddamn it!" shouted Garner wearily, and threw down his hat. "You sonofabitch, you did it again!"

Hobie had dismounted too. "Boss?"" he said. "Front legs."

"I saw, I saw," Garner snapped. "That damned idiot rode her right into the ground anyway you look at it."

"Where'd he come 'cross her, anyways?"

Garner didn't answer. There was probably a dead traveler somewhere up north of them, someplace outside Half Moon Crossing, for Belasco couldn't have been headed anywhere else. Dead traveler or not, though, Garner had to keep on the trail. He couldn't help the pinto's owner, but he could sure as hell track down Belasco. He was close now, he knew it.

This poor, dead mare, more than anything else, reinforced the feeling he'd had that it was, indeed, Belasco he'd heard galloping past them last night. Oh, he trusted his hunches, all right. He hadn't lived this long without learning to listen to that quiet voice inside, the one that alerted him to danger.

Of course it hadn't alerted him to Hobie's sneaking up on him a couple of times in the past few days. But then, Hobie wasn't exactly danger, was he?

And then, quite suddenly, he grew cold.

"Shit," he muttered, and snatched up Faro's reins. "Marcus Trevor and that damned reporter are behind us. I'll bet Belasco's heading straight for them, and he's lookin' for a fresh mount." He swung up on Faro. "You'd best hope Marcus's even a worse tracker than you thought, Hobie."

Hobie, looking worried, scrambled into Fly's saddle. The sun blasting low over their left shoulders, they set off at a hard gallop.

Marcus Trevor was dead and already beginning to draw flies. They buzzed thickly at his neck, where Belasco had cleanly severed his jugular with one stroke and thus ended his life. They wandered over his open eyes, inside his breathless nostrils.

They crawled over Woolsey's ears, too, or rather, the places where his ears had been, tickling, itching, biting, scratching raw flesh.

Feeding.

Belasco hadn't killed Woolsey, although Woolsey wished that he had. He'd passed out when he saw that razor flashing near, passed out like a girl, he thought with shame. And when he'd wakened to a world of throbbing pain, he'd found himself hog-tied, with both his bloody, severed ears placed neatly on his chest. That, and a note written in his own blood on his own notepad.

"Hear no evil," it read.

He had fainted again, then, and had passed in and out of consciousness ever since.

He pulled against his bonds once more, only to feel a new, bright surge of pain shoot through his head and replace the throbbing with fresh fire.

He cried out, despite himself.

It was hopeless. Utterly hopeless. The sun was barely up, and already he could see the vultures circling overhead.

He shook his head, hoping to discourage some of the damned flies, then twisted and, gritting his teeth, pressed the raw wound down into the desert floor. He cried out again, this time through tightly clenched teeth, then repeated the grisly process for the other ear, coating the wound with dirt and sealing it from the flies' ministrations.

He was reasonably certain he wouldn't have time to die from the infection he'd probably just picked up. The sun and the vultures would kill him first. But he'd be damned if he was going to die with his ears full of wriggling, hatching maggots.

That would be too awful to contemplate.

He passed out again.

Grimly, Garner stepped down off his horse, then moved forward, shooing away the alighting buzzards. Hobie remained mounted, his hand covering his mouth to hold in the shriek he was terrified would emerge if he gave it a chance.

Dead. Both Deputy Marcus Trevor and Mr. Clive

Woolsey, dead as a couple of hogs at butchering time, and both covered in blood.

This wouldn't have happened if he hadn't deserted them, Hobie thought. He never should have ridden out of High Draw alone, no matter how he felt about the company. He should have stayed with them, seen it through instead of taking off to catch up with Garner and have some excitement.

Well, he'd had about enough excitement to last several lifetimes. First Martindale, and now this. It wasn't as gruesome, but it was just as final. And it was his fault, his fault alone. If he could have traded places with them, he would have.

A sob escaped him.

"Help me, kid," Garner said.

Hobie sat his horse, not moving.

"I said help me, dammit," Garner repeated curtly. He knelt down beside Woolsey's body and rested his palm on the reporter's chest, then grabbed him by his hair and turned his head. "He's still alive."

Belasco rode the gray nearly into the ground, but he made the far southern hills. He rode the gray as high as he could, then tethered him, head down and lathered, and climbed the rest of the way up the rocky, crumbling ground on tired hands and aching knees. Then he pulled out his spyglass and had a good look around at the flatlands that spread below him.

Nothing but a couple of coyotes hunting a rabbit. A few birds.

No one.

Relaxing at last, he leaned back into a pool of deep shadow and allowed his eyes to flutter closed. If he'd ridden too close to that camp last night, no one had woken. And if they had, well, he'd given them someone to bury instead of following him. He was reasonably certain they'd have to stop to bury someone so impressive as a U.S. deputy marshal.

He smirked.

He fumbled for his pocket and opened his eyes long enough to look at the badge he'd taken off that long-haired Nancy-boy's body. He held it out so that it glistened in the sun.

Lovely, he thought, tucking it away again and closing his eyes once more. Real silver. Doubtless this little darling would come in quite handy in the future.

It came to him that he stank of days on the run, stank of blood still on his clothing, blood that had belonged to Martindale and the deputy and that ridiculous reporter.

"Ridiculous and earless, now," he muttered, and chuckled. It was a dry, rattling sound that sent a wren he hadn't seen, perched just overhead, to flight.

He was too tired to jump.

I should probably climb back down and water that creature, he thought. I should probably have a wash, myself.

He didn't move, though, except to pull his makeshift body armor from under his clothing. Murchison's Apparel skidded down the slope, followed by Camden's Ague Remedy. Good riddance, he thought. He wouldn't need them now. He felt pounds lighter and ten degrees cooler.

He fell straight into an exhausted sleep.

Hobie lugged another armful of rocks back to the camp, dropped them beside the cairn, then mopped his brow. It was going to take a little while longer—and a lot more rocks—before they had Deputy Trevor safely

tucked away. His boots and lower legs were still uncovered in the shallow grave they'd made for him.
They'd have to pile the rocks deep to keep the coyotes
and such away from the body until somebody could
come to take his body home.

Beside him, Garner knelt on the ground, shifting into
place the rocks Hobie had brought.

"Sit down, boy," Garner said. He sounded as exhausted as Hobie felt. "Take a break. Drink some
water."

There was no argument from Hobie. He slouched a
few feet over to one side and sank to the ground. He
landed beside the prone Woolsey, whose head was
wrapped in the last tatters of Garner's new shirt and the
late Deputy Trevor's spare butternuts. On either side of
Woolsey's head, blood flowered and soaked the bandages in bright red blooms.

"That was pretty smart of you, Mr. Woolsey," Hobie
said between gulps of water, "rollin' your ears in the dirt
like that."

And then he realized he'd said "ears," and started to
apologize for maybe bringing up bad memories, except
that Woolsey held up a hand—the one that wasn't
cradling his head—and breathed, "Shut up. Just shut
up."

"Might want to give him another slug of that laudanum, Hobie," Garner grunted, and settled another big
rock into place. You couldn't put the little ones on top,
he'd told Hobie. Too easy for the vermin to move. No,
you had to pack it just so, with the big rocks covering
most everything and the little ones in between, and then
big ones over the top again.

"Yessir," Hobie said, and got up to rifle through Garner's saddlebags again. He found the little brown glass bottle after a few seconds, and took it to Woolsey.

Woolsey accepted it without a word.

"Easy!" said Hobie when Woolsey appeared ready to drain the bottle. He snatched it back. "You gotta save some for later."

Woolsey wiped his mouth. "Filthy-tasting stuff," he muttered. And then he looked over at Hobie and said, "Why should I save any? It can't possibly get any worse than it is right at this moment."

"Sure it can," said Garner. He stood up, put his hands in the small of his back, and stretched. Hobie didn't think he'd ever seen Garner so tired. He seemed to have a whole flock of new lines around those dark blue eyes, and weariness tugged at the corners of his mouth.

"Hand me that canteen," he said, and Hobie did. Garner tilted it back and took a long drink, and then, with just a hint of a smile, said to Woolsey, "Remember, you gotta be fit enough to ride that mule again. And we're settin' off pretty soon."

Woolsey dropped his head to his knees. "No," he cried softly. "No."

"Yeah," said Garner, and tossed the canteen to Hobie. "Two more loads, boy," he said, and walked away, picking up rocks as he went.

"Yessir," Hobie said. He put down the canteen and started lugging rocks.

Woolsey wished somebody would kill him. Damn that Belasco for making him into a caricature of a man, for making him into an earless freak! Garner had assured him he'd live, but it was no comfort, no comfort at all. What woman would keep company with him now?

He couldn't even keep his glasses on anymore. He'd

tried putting them on, but they slithered down the raw
places where his ears had been, causing him as much
frustration as agony. He only had them on now because
the earpieces were threaded through– and held in place
by– the bandages Garner had wrapped him in.

He supposed the only woman that would have him
now would be that appalling little prostitute back in
High Draw. And even she had one more ear than he did.

Garner's laudanum had helped ease his misery somewhat, but now he was riding this horrid hell-beast of a
mule again. There seemed no escaping it. He couldn't
even die, and thus get away. And away– far, far
away– he certainly wanted to be. Anywhere. Anywhere
but on this miserable creature chasing a madman that he
didn't want to catch, that he never wanted to hear of
again.

Oh, God, why hadn't he just stayed in Tucson? Tucson wasn't so bad, was it? At least there were restaurants and dance halls, and stage plays that came through
with some regularity. At least everyone there had ears
still on their heads and not in their pockets.

He touched his jacket momentarily, feeling the soft
resistance of thin cartilage through fabric. He supposed
he should have buried them back there, where they'd
left Trevor. But he couldn't bring himself to take them
out and put them in the dirt.

Neither could he bring himself to reach in and take
them out and look at them.

At least the mule hadn't tried to bite him again.

He wondered if it knew, if it felt sorry for him. Oh,
that would just be the end, wouldn't it, if this hideous
beast felt sorry for him!

And what on earth did Garner intend to do when he
caught up with Belasco? The fiend could just as easily

creep into camp again and kill them all. Or worse, cut off their ears and let them live.

No, there was worse than that. Hobie had confided to him the condition in which the late Vincent Martindale had been found. Woolsey shuddered violently, just thinking about it. Belasco had already severed Woolsey's ears. He didn't like to think what Belasco would cut off next time.

As he rode along behind Garner and Hobie, through this godless man-eater of a landscape, Woolsey began to silently weep.

19

The day stretched on. Four hours' sleep wasn't enough for an old man, Garner thought. There had been days, long ago, when he could have forsaken all sleep for twenty-four, even forty-eight hours at a time. And had. But those days were long in his past.

He took some solace that Hobie kept falling asleep in the saddle. He didn't know about Woolsey. He only glanced back at him occasionally, just to make sure he was still there.

It was a damn shame about Woolsey. Garner had met men similarly disfigured before: men with no nose, men with their lips cut or bitten off in bar fights, men with odd chunks of their bodies sawed or chewed or sliced away. Usually, they'd been drunk and wild when it happened. He'd known a few carved-up, chewed-up, burnt-up fellows that had been victims of Indians, too.

But it was a damn shame about Woolsey. He didn't belong out here in the first place, but now he'd been permanently marked by it. The loss of those ears wouldn't have been so bad if he'd been, say, some old logger from up north who never went to town, never planned to, and had scant interest in a woman's company.

Garner shook his head. Woolsey had better stay out West, where the women were a little less choosy. He'd best look into getting himself some of those little nose-hugging glasses, the kind that didn't need ear-bars, and he'd better keep his hair as long as it was now, too, and for the rest of his life. At least you didn't notice anything straight off.

"Hobie?" he said.

He heard the sound of hoofbeats, hurrying to catch up. Fly's bobbing buckskin head, then Hobie's blond one, appeared next to his shoulder. "Yeah, Boss?"

"I figure we'll make those hills in about an hour," Garner said, pointing. Belasco's trail headed straight for them. "We'll stop and rest once we get there. How's the water holding out?"

"Still got about half my bag and one canteen," the boy said, and Garner could hear the exhaustion in his voice. "Woolsey's out of canteen water, but his bag's maybe three-quarters full."

Garner was in about the same shape as Hobie as far as water was concerned. He said, "Fine. We're in decent shape."

"What if he's layin' up there, waitin' for us?" Hobie asked.

Garner shook his head. "Not this one. He's a bad shot at any distance. Least he was when I knew him, and I doubt he's had much chance to practice in Yuma Prison. He's gonna try to outrun us, so long as Trevor's horse holds out."

"Can we catch him in a day and a half?" Hobie asked. He knew how far the water would go, too.

"I reckon," Garner said. "I reckon we'll catch up with him today. Trevor's horse is damn good, but he's got to be as tired as these." He patted Faro's neck. "Plus which, Belasco's got no sense about horses. Got no sense about the desert, either. He's a town boy. He'll make mistakes, and those mistakes'll slow him down."

"Today?" Hobie swallowed so hard that Garner saw his Adam's apple bob wildly.

Garner said, "Did you think we were just going to chase the little bastard forever?"

Hobie didn't say anything.

Garner figured that once they reached the hills, he'd give Hobie and Woolsey the option of staying put while he rode on up. Woolsey would be a distinct liability up there, and besides, he had no business tracking a killer like Belasco in the first place.

And Hobie?

Hobie should have stayed home, too.

Garner had selfishly let him tag along because he'd been happy for the company, let him tag along on a trip that might easily cost him his life. It had surely cost Marcus Trevor dearly. As disgusted as Garner had been with Trevor's flash and showmanship and antics, he pitied the man who'd have to tell Annie Trevor that she was a widow.

His arm hurt beneath the bandages, and he started to rub it. But that made it worse, and he took his hand away and snorted. That bartender back in High Draw just had to be a goddamn Farley. It just figured.

Oh, he was having lots of luck this time out, all of it bad. First Hobie had followed him, and then they'd gotten suckered in by Marcus Trevor and his personal reporter. Then they'd been too late to save those poor folks back outside Baker.

He could count the incidents of bad luck on his fingers, all right, and use them all up. He just hoped the last piece of ill fortune wouldn't be Belasco's razor in his neck. Or someplace more tender.

He found himself thinking of old Pike, his former partner, and wishing he was here with him right now. Pike had known what Garner was thinking before Garner knew it himself. Pike could sure drive you looney, but he'd been a crazy old bastard, completely without fear. He would have ridden right into the mouth of hell itself just to see what it was like, and he would have gone in with that lopsided grin on his face, too.

But Pike's dead and you're not riding into hell, Garner reminded himself. You're riding up there to put a bullet in Belasco's brain.

He decided that he wouldn't offer Hobie and Woolsey the option of staying put. He'd insist on it. Belasco was a smart little prick, but Garner figured to be just a little bit smarter.

He'd better not mess with Marcus's horse, he thought belatedly.

If he found that gray of Trevor's at the wayside with its throat cut, he wouldn't shoot Belasco in the head. He'd insert the bullet by hand.

Belasco limped painfully up yet another rugged hill, leading the gray. There was no vegetation to speak of, no shelter. The footing was poor and his boots skidded on the rocky soil every few steps, and his hip was hurting again. Sometimes he caught himself on the side of the horse or the saddle; sometimes he went down all the way to his knees, cursing.

Louder when he landed on his bad hip. The pain from it completely overwhelmed any argument his shallow-shot back was giving him.

This could all have been avoided if he'd just stayed awake long enough to water the bloody nag, he thought. When he woke with the sun beating on his face, he'd raced down to it and watered it then, watered it more than enough, but it still wasn't acting right. He'd tried riding it for a while, then gotten off and started walking and leading it.

He'd lost two horses in the last twenty-four hours. He wasn't going to take a chance on losing another, especially since it was the last one available.

Even now, he could hear the horse's belly sounds, a squish-swish-squish-swish. Maybe it was normal. He didn't think so, though. He'd never paid much attention to a horse's belly before.

He slipped and fell to his knees again. This time, he didn't make his hip worse, but he ripped his britches. He swore under his breath. Bad enough that he was most probably being pursued, but did he have to destroy his wardrobe, too?

He stood up, brushed himself off, and inspected his knee, which was scraped and oozing blood beneath the torn fabric. It stung like the devil, and when he touched it, he hissed in air through his teeth.

"This is ridiculous, positively ludicrous," he muttered, and looked about. He was nearly up to the crest of a saddle of arid land between two high, crumbling hills. He thought he might have a fairly decent vantage point once he got up a tad higher. If he couldn't spot anyone following him from up there, then he could stop, make camp, and have a decent rest. Perhaps this stupid horse would stop making those sounds, too.

"Come along, fellow," he said, gave a tug on the reins, and started limping and skidding his way up the hill again. For every two steps up he took, he slithered back one.

A little better than a half hour later, he was up to the saddle of land, which was relatively flat ground in a region of hard angles. He ground-tied the gray, then went back and weighted the reins with a rock, just to be on the safe side.

It wasn't necessary. The gray just stood there listlessly, head down.

Spyglass tucked firmly in his pocket, Belasco began to climb up the easternmost slope. It was rough going, but within about fifteen minutes he had reached a point where he could get a good look out over the flatlands below.

Slowly sweeping from side to side, he moved the spyglass over the flat.

Nothing, nothing, nothing.

A grin began to spread over his face.

Closer and closer.

Still nothing.

He'd gotten away, clean as the proverbial whistle, free as the proverbial Scot.

And then his grin suddenly faded.

There, right there at the base of the farthest hill, just coming into the shade: three riders, and one of them was that stupid, newly-earless reporter on his stupid mule, the one Belasco had thought beneath killing. Seething, he watched as they got down off their mounts, loosened their saddles, sat down in the shade of a steep outcrop, and passed a canteen.

No, not all of them. The biggest one—didn't he look

slightly familiar?—stayed with the horses, divvying out water, waiting while they drank.

And then the strangest feeling came over him. He leaned forward, staring through the glass. They were so far away. . . .

No, it couldn't be, could it? All these years . . .

He pulled the glass away from his eye, rubbed at it with the one piece of shirttail that wasn't spotted with blood or dirt or both, and raised it to his eye again.

That sheriff. The one from Medicine Rock. What was his name? He'd heard it enough times.

Garner. Sheriff King Garner.

Not possible. It had been years and years, after all, and as he remembered, Garner was no spring chicken even then. Although his perception of Garner, Belasco thought, might have been tempered by his own age.

But this man, like Garner, was certainly taller than most. He was built like Garner had been—broad-chested, slim-hipped—and there was something familiar about the way he carried himself, something cocksure, something that made Belasco's blood boil.

And when the man took off his hat to wipe his brow, exposing that short, thick mop of dark hair, Belasco was certain.

"Hail fellow well met, indeed," he whispered, for the very first time just a little frightened. He remembered being trucked for days over the back of a horse, like an unwelcome sack of produce. Garner had not spoken one civil word to him in all the time it took to get from Phoenix to Prescott, nearly five days. The extent of his conversation, in fact, had been "Hold still, dammit," and "You gotta shit, do it now."

Then, of course, there had been the trial to concentrate on, and that had been so entertaining that he hadn't given Garner another thought. Not much of one, anyway.

He didn't breathe as he watched Garner sit down with the others in the deep shade. "Sonofabitch," Belasco muttered, then collapsed the spyglass with a snap of the palm of his hand. "Goddamn pernicious, everlasting sonofabitch. You're trying to do it again! Slap baby's hand and send him to his room."

But then a smile slowly crept over his features until it overtook them.

"Daddy, oh, Daddy," he said in a soft, singsong fashion. "Daddy's coming home." He stuck the spyglass down in his pocket. He adjusted his position so that his hip didn't hurt so much, leaned back against a rock, and ran his fingers gently over another pocket, the pocket that held his razor.

"Does Daddy want to play with something shiny, something sharp?"

Garner slumped down between Woolsey and Hobie and took his turn with the canteen. He drained it, then handed it to Hobie.

"Don't look up," he said quietly.

And then Hobie surprised him by asking, "You see it, too, Boss?"

"See what?" asked Woolsey thickly. "Do you have any more of that laudanum? I could use a bit."

They both ignored him.

"Up top?" Garner asked. "The saddle between the two big hills?"

Hobie nodded. "A couple flashes of light. You reckon he's got him a spyglass?"

"Either that or he's polishing that blade of his."

Woolsey suddenly seemed to make sense of the conversation. In fact, he had a physical reaction to it, in the form of a clumsy leap to his feet and a lunge toward the horses.

Garner yanked him back into a sit, growling, "Settle down, man!"

"He's up there!" the earless Woolsey cried, and his voice was thin with hysteria. Any trace of his stupor had vanished, at least for the time being. "He's watching us!"

Garner grabbed Woolsey's arm before it could swing up and point, and snarled, "You pull that again, you little peckerwood, and I'm gonna finish up what Belasco started on you, you got that?"

Woolsey jerked his arm back and rubbed at it.

"You can't keep those hands down, sit on 'em," Garner added. And then, somewhat cruelly, he added, "Besides, I thought you wanted to get your story."

"That's kinda low, Boss," Hobie whispered from behind him. "I mean what with . . . what with everythin' that's happened to him."

"Kill your own snakes, Hobie," Garner snapped, and then felt bad for it. He didn't say so, though. It wasn't in him to know how. He just frowned, then got to the business of thinking what to do next.

Belasco was up there, sure as the sun rose in the east. All Garner had to figure out now was how to get to him. It would take a lot of figuring.

Belasco could be a tricky little bastard. If they went up after him in full view, he was just as liable to set an ambush as make a run for it, and the odds were fifty-fifty that he'd double back and try to pick them off, one at a time, from behind. Close up and sneaky, that was how Belasco liked to work.

There was no getting away from the fact that he knew

they were here, and knew there were three of them. Garner already knew that Belasco didn't consider Woolsey any threat at all. If he had, he'd be dead right now instead of just minus his head-handles.

Belasco would have no way of rating Hobie, an unknown. And Garner didn't believe that Belasco was close enough, even with that spyglass, to have recognized *him.*

He just wished that he wasn't so goddamned tired. He'd think better. The only thing keeping him halfway sharp was his bullet-scraped arm.

"What next, Boss?" Hobie asked after a time.

"Let me cogitate on it a little longer," said a weary Garner, and dipped fingers into his pocket for his fixings. "He's not goin' anywhere."

"How do you know that?" Woolsey hissed. "How could you possibly know? And how can you smoke at a time like this?"

Garner shook out tobacco into a V-shaped paper, then tucked the pouch back into his pocket. "He's not gonna move until we do." With his free hand, he picked up a handful of powdery earth and released it. It billowed high and full. "See that? If he did, his horse'd kick up enough dust to let us know somebody was up there, and he'd have to figure we'd be on him like syrup on flapjacks. No, he'll stay right where he is until we force him to move."

He gave the cigarette a final lick and a twist, stuck it in his mouth, and struck a match. Around it, he added, "Not that it's any of your damn business, but I think better when I smoke."

20

Why weren't they moving? And why in the world had he thrown away that bloody makeshift body armor?

Belasco hadn't budged since he'd first sighted the trio. They were faint specks at this distance, but faint specks that could easily have been part of the landscape. Even though he could just barely make them out, he'd pulled out his spyglass over and over to check.

An hour! An hour and they hadn't moved! What was keeping them?

And then he had a positively sterling thought. What if they weren't going to come after him? What if this range of hills was simply too daunting for them? After all, they couldn't have much more water than he. They had actually given up, and were simply resting their horses and themselves for the long journey back from whence they'd come!

Cowards!

But his grin faded as soon as it had bloomed. If they

were planning on staying put, why hadn't they made camp? They were just sitting there in the shade. The big one in the middle—the one he'd convinced himself was that blasted Sheriff King Garner—was smoking every now and then, and from time to time they passed a canteen back and forth, but that was it. Not one of them had so much as stood up and stretched.

They had to know he'd come in here. He'd been in such a hurry that he hadn't taken any pains to cover his tracks. Perhaps they were frightened to come further!

Now, that was a thought. Maybe they were arguing about it. Come to think of it, he had seen that earless idiot gesturing quite strenuously.

But the big sheriff would be all for it, Belasco thought with a sneer. Oh, that one would want his blood and nothing short of it.

And the other two? The reporter was a frightened little bird of a fellow, no two ways about it. And the third one, the wee blonde? Well, he was a question mark. But neither was he big, nor did he look to be seasoned. He was little more than a boy. Those two were probably voting to go back home to the safety of their parlors, Belasco decided.

But Garner, even by himself, posed a problem.

Belasco ground his teeth. He couldn't even sneak away. It might be green with spring on the flatland— well, as green as possible considering the locale—but up here it was hot and dry, with no plant life whatsoever to hold down the dust. If he attempted to walk that beast the thirty-odd feet to get to the downhill slope, he'd raise enough dust to be seen for miles and miles.

His earlier bravado had been weakened somewhat by the heat of the climbing sun, and the fact that he was nearly out of water.

He should have picked up extra water when he killed that deputy, he thought. He shouldn't have given so much of what little he had taken to the horse. The horse wasn't grateful. All the damn thing did was make hideous sounds in its belly.

Belasco would have been thrilled to wash out his clothes. Filthy rags! As it was, there was hardly enough to drink.

Which reminded him, he was thirsty.

He gave a final stare through the glass at the faraway trio of men. Still sitting there, still smoking, still conversing. Then he collapsed the glass, slipped it back into his pocket, and slithered—very slowly and carefully, so as not to raise any dust—back down the hill.

Fifteen minutes later, after creeping back up to his perch, Belasco raised the spyglass to his eye again.

He lowered it, blinked, then raised it once more.

"Damn and blast!" he muttered.

Two of them. The two pups. No Garner, and Garner's horse was missing, too. There was no dust trail leading away from the place he'd been, so the only way he could have gone was into the range of hills, toward Belasco. Obviously, he was hidden from view by the undulating surface of the ground.

Panic set in, but was just as suddenly replaced, Belasco thought proudly, by the clicking of his logical mind. Why should he run from this pompous, overgrown saddle tramp? Why indeed, when there were two pigeons down there, ripe for the plucking and all alone with nobody to protect them?

He could circle back, have a little fun, then wait for Garner. He could even up a very old score. There'd be plenty of water, plenty enough for a lazy ride down into Mexico with no one hounding him.

Smiling, he shinnied down the slope, not caring how much dust he raised this time, and limped to the gray. "Sick or not," he whispered, swinging painfully up into the saddle, "noises or not, you are going to carry me, old fellow."

Without a care for the clouds of dust he kicked up, he took off across the saddle of arid land. But instead of following the more reasonable path—which would have been down the slope and south, toward Mexico—he made a hard left turn. Riding at angles, he began to circumnavigate the hill he'd climbed, circling carefully back toward those two lonesome cowpokes.

As he climbed deeper into the hills, Garner was hoping that damn Woolsey wouldn't cave in and do something stupid. He knew he could trust Hobie, all right. He'd do what he was told, and do it the best he could. He was that kind of kid. But Woolsey was another matter.

They gone over it three times. Garner would ride up into the hills. Belasco, having seen him, would likely start to run. But then, knowing Belasco, he'd think twice on it. He'd want to get rid of them once and for all, and then take a leisurely trip down south of the border, not a hurried one with trouble on his tail.

And so he'd pick them off. He'd probably leave Garner for last. First, because Garner would be the one to ride up there after him. And second, because he'd have had to recognize Woolsey—the bandages and the mule would do it if nothing else did—and realize he was no threat.

Woolsey had objected at this point, but glares from Hobie and Garner had settled him pretty quickly.

Which left Hobie as the only possible danger down

the hill. And even Hobie admitted he didn't look like much—from far off or close up, either one.

So Garner would ride far enough up the range to convince Belasco that he was coming. And Belasco—Garner believed this for all he was worth—would try to circle back and take out Hobie and Woolsey.

Again, Woolsey had objected.

"You'll not use me for . . . for bait!" he'd cried. "I'm no worm on a fishing line!"

"You are now," Hobie had said. "Now, shut the heck up."

When all of this started, Garner had been unsure of the boy. Unsure, in fact, if he even liked him. Too much hero worship for his taste, especially when he wasn't any hero. But now, by God, he was almost to the point of admiring him.

Almost.

Woolsey had shut up, and now Garner was riding forward. He planned to travel for perhaps a half hour. He figured it would take Belasco at least three times that long to circle around to where Hobie and Woolsey were waiting. Garner would slip back, hide up in the rocks, and when Belasco came in after Hobie and Woolsey, he'd fire.

And that would be the end of it.

It seemed a rather unpoetic end for Belasco—not that he deserved anything better—but at least it was final. A real period on the end of the sentence. And that was all that Garner was after. He already knew where he'd perch and wait. On that little ledge, just above the place where they'd stopped. It looked like there was clear access to it.

He'd never been up there, exactly, but he'd been through this range countless times years before, and as he remembered, there was probably enough room for a man to scramble that high on his belly, and a narrow slit in the rocks below where he could hide Faro.

So he rode on, slowly climbing into the graveled, sere, dead-brown hills, just waiting for the time when he could turn around and start circling back.

And kill Belasco once and for all.

Belasco finally came to a relatively flat space in a world full of angles and dangerous slopes. He reined in his horse and sat there, working his jaw back and forth.

When he'd come up with this plan, he'd only perceived that Garner had split up with the other two.

He hadn't asked himself if there could be any ulterior motives to this.

Now he asked.

Garner might believe those two would prove liabilities in a tussle. He was most probably correct about that, by the look of them. But if so, why had he ridden all this way with them in the first place? Or rather, with the young blonde, Belasco thought, correcting himself. The reporter hadn't been with them. He'd been with that long-haired deputy.

All right, the reporter was a rescue, picked up on the fly. But that other young fellow must have something on the ball for Garner to have brought him.

So why leave him behind at this late date?

Why not simply leave the reporter alone and come up after him with two guns instead of one?

And then Belasco's eyes narrowed.

"Tut-tut, Sheriff Garner," he whispered. "Up to your old tricks, I see."

He reined the gray—who had stopped making those horrible belly noises—to the right, and rode him up the slope high enough that he had a fair view of the terrain. Not high enough to spot Garner, but adequate to roughly gauge the lay of the land.

He made a mental note of where he imagined Garner must be right about now, and where the youngsters were waiting, and the quickest, most circumspect route to where he wanted to go.

It was roundabout, but it would do, he thought. It would most probably do splendidly.

He set out on his new course.

21

"This is ridiculous," Woolsey said yet again. Hobie had lost count. "I'm grievously injured, I'm in pain, and I'm leaving while I can. And you can keep your blasted horse. The mule will do me quite nicely, thank you."

He started to rise.

Exasperated, Hobie pulled his side arm and cocked it. Woolsey froze at the sound.

"Sit back down, Mr. Woolsey," Hobie said in a cold, emotionless tone that, whether he knew it or not, mimicked Garner's. "Do it now."

Woolsey eased back. "Don't be silly," he said, although the cracking in his voice made his words somewhat unconvincing.

Hobie eased the hammer back down, but didn't lower the gun. "Look, Mr. Woolsey," he said. "I know you don't want to be here. I don't wanna be here, either. But we are, and that's what matters. You gotta do like the boss says. You gotta trust him."

Woolsey sniffed. "And look how well that's done for me so far. I am permanently maimed! I'm a freak!"

Behind Woolsey's haughty front, Hobie knew there was a man close to tears. He couldn't say that he blamed him. But he said, "That happened 'cause you were trustin' in the wrong man. I'm sorry to say it, but there it is. I kinda liked Deputy Trevor myself, especially at the beginning, but he made a big mistake comin' out here in the first place."

"As did we all," muttered Woolsey.

"I reckon," said Hobie thoughtfully. "All of us, 'cept maybe Mr. Garner."

Woolsey sniffed. "He's going to end up just as dead as the rest of us."

Hobie holstered his gun. "I wouldn't be countin' my chicks just yet, Mr. Woolsey." He pulled out his pocket watch and stared at it, then put it away. The hairs were prickling the back of his neck. He'd been hanging around Garner too long, he supposed, because he was having one of those feelings. One of those Garner feelings.

And it wasn't good.

Garner found a narrow pass between hills and reined Faro to the south and through it. From this point onward, he'd be hidden from prying eyes, even those with a spyglass, because he'd be shielded by hills the rest of the way. It was for this reason that he'd come as far as he had.

The pass cut down deep, narrowed, then widened again, almost into a shallow canyon with an uneven floor. He had to go carefully, for although Faro was surefooted, the substrate was uncertain at best. It crumbled away just when you didn't suspect it. It slid to the right or the left, smack out from under shod hooves, and parts of it were steep to boot.

He kept contact with the horse's mouth, feeling the ground through him, and spoke in a soothing tone, saying, "There, boy," and, "Easy, old son, that's the way." This wasn't a place a horse would choose to go through, even if he wasn't burdened with a rider. Garner didn't particularly want to go through it either, but there you were.

At last the pass held level for a bit, although it curved to the east, then the south, then the east again. Faro relaxed, but not Garner. He watched the crags ahead of him on either side, on alert for any puff of dust, any dislodged pebbles that would betray Belasco's presence.

He began to get one of those feelings of his again, a gnawing that something wasn't right. He reined in Faro and sat there for a minute. Nothing. No sound but the light wind whistling softly through the rocks. There wasn't even a bird in sight.

Still, something intangible disturbed him. He sat and waited a while longer, drew his gun, then holstered it in disgust.

Too long on the trail, he thought with a shake of his head. Too long without sleep.

When he got back home, he was going pack his damn arm in ice and sleep for a week.

He clucked to Faro, and the horse moved out at a slow walk toward the next hard turn in the pass's floor.

Suddenly, the horse's ears came to full attention. Garner stopped him short. Faro had heard something, all right. Garner sat here a time, waiting, listening.

Nothing.

"You're gettin' as bad as me," he finally said to the bay. "Jumping at shadows."

Again, he clucked to the horse.

He rounded what appeared to be the final turn before he'd have to climb again. This stretch of the pass was about twenty feet wide, and short: only thirty feet long before it ended in a soft rise.

He was riding down the middle of it when something fell from the sky and knocked him off the gelding's back.

He knew it was Belasco before he hit the ground.

Belasco clung to his back like a monkey, and Garner saw the razor swooping, arcing down toward his throat when he was still in the air.

Faro shied to the side. Garner gripped Belasco's arm just before they hit the ground, hit it so hard it jarred Garner's teeth.

It didn't do his arm much good, either.

There was no time to think about it, even to cry out in pain. There was only time to try to get the damn razor out of Belasco's hand.

Garner had hold of his wrist, hard, but Belasco wasn't dropping the blade. Garner mustered all his strength and suddenly twisted onto his back, hoping to pin the sonofabitch beneath him. But Belasco somehow wiggled out from under him and managed to get the hand with the razor free.

Garner leapt to his feet, but no faster than Belasco. Garner took a hop back and reached for his gun.

It wasn't there.

Belasco held it in his other hand, twirling it on his index finger. "Looking for this, Sheriff darling?"

Garner held his ground. "You're a mess, Belasco," he said, panting. "What happened to those pretty-boy looks?"

Belasco stopped twirling the gun. He stood a tad

straighter, although with a slight hitch, and looked a little peeved. "Oh, they're here, my good Sheriff Garner. They're here beneath these filthy rags."

"I'm not a sheriff anymore," Garner said, stalling for time. Was Belasco favoring that hip just a touch?

"Ah, retired. You're a good bit older, too, than last we met," Belasco replied. He tossed Garner's gun over his shoulder, toward the base of the rise. He cocked his head. "I'm curious. If you're not in the pay of some local government or other, why on earth did you desert your rocking chair—I'm assuming you have one—to come after me?"

Garner ground his teeth. "Because you were mine," he said finally.

"And that was all?" Belasco asked. "My goodness! We are the proprietary sort, aren't we?"

Garner ignored the comment. "You tossed my gun over there, so I reckon you don't want to shoot me. You going to try to slice me up like you did Martindale?"

Belasco smiled and adjusted his stance slightly. "You found him, did you? Well, something like. And there's no 'try' to it. You're rather old, my friend. Older than I had imagined. Doubtless you're slow, too. Oh, don't worry, I like that in an opponent. By the time I'm finished with you, my dear Garner, you'll look like you fell into a threshing machine."

Garner just stood there, jaw muscles working.

"Nothing to say?" Belasco said. "Well, I'm not surprised, not really. You never were the talkative sort, as I remember."

Suddenly, Belasco lunged toward him, lunged with that razor slashing.

Garner jumped to the left, arms before his face, and he felt a new sting along his left forearm as Belasco missed his face. His sleeve flapping, Garner moved forward again while Belasco's momentum was still taking him around, and kicked him in that bad hip just as hard as he could.

Belasco let out a shout and fell forward. Garner threw himself right on top of him. But Belasco managed to twist over before the whole of Garner's weight hit him, and made another swing with the razor.

This time, it scored the side of Garner's neck. Not deeply, but deeply enough that Belasco laughed, a short triumphant bark that began the next swing of his arm.

Garner blocked it with his elbow and Belasco caught nothing but air.

"Damn you!" Belasco roared.

Garner dropped the point of his shoulder into Belasco's chest and made a grab for the hand that held the razor. He caught it by the wrist.

"Not so easy as it looks, is it, when it's not a gal and it's not hog-tied?" he panted through gritted teeth.

Before Belasco had a chance to do more than open his mouth, Garner yanked just as hard as he could on Belasco's wrist, burying the corner of the razor in Belasco's throat.

A look of shocked surprise passed over Belasco's face.

But before Garner could drag the blade deeper, Belasco somehow mustered inhuman strength and rolled away, slithered like an eel. Before Garner could blink, Belasco was up on his feet, blood spattering from his neck in little spurts and the razor handle jutting from it.

Garner made a lunge for him, but Belasco only had a couple of feet to travel before Garner's gun was in his hand. Garner froze, less than six feet away.

"Hate to do it," Belasco said hoarsely, thickly. "Out

of character, you know." He touched his throat, and blood bubbled against his fingers. "And I am very much afraid you've taken me with you. Ah, well."

He smiled suddenly, completely ingenuously, then pointed the gun directly at the middle of Garner's forehead.

A single shot rang out.

Except that Garner was still standing, and Belasco, a puzzled look on his face, was pitching forward. He landed on the razor, effectively finishing the job Garner had started. Garner watched the wound gush two huge surges of blood before Belasco's heart stopped.

"What the . . . ?" Garner mumbled.

"You okay, Boss?" Hobie shouted from down the pass. He was just sticking his rifle back in its boot. Behind him, Woolsey's bandaged head warily peeked around a large rock.

With a plop, Garner sat down where he stood. He was breathing hard, and his shirt was bright with blood, both his and Belasco's. He felt the long slice on his neck when the blade had caught him. Jagged. Probably leave a scar. But it wasn't bleeding too awful bad. Neither was the cut in his forearm. They both stung like bastards, though, and his shirt was sure as hell ruined.

"What in Hades are you doing up here?" he belatedly roared at Hobie, who was riding up, Woolsey and the surefoot Charlie Blue in his wake. "Thought I told you to wait."

"Sorry, Boss," said Hobie, getting down off Fly. "We did wait. For a while. Reckon I'll just take my bullet back out of him and ride on down the slope." He looked at Garner's arm, then his neck. "You gonna live?" His eyes flicked to Belasco, as if to make certain he was dead.

"Reckon," Garner said, and grunting, pushed himself

up off the ground. "And you didn't kill him. Don't go get-tin' ideas and having nightmares and such. I stuck that blade into his throat, and it was the blade that did him in."

Hobie blinked. It could have been either in relief or disappointment, but Garner figured it was relief. Hobie was just a boy. He didn't need to start his adulthood off thinking that he'd killed a man, even if it was a barely human man like Belasco.

"Well, I slowed him down, didn't I?" Hobie asked.

Garner nodded. "Yup. You sure did." He stepped over to the corpse.

"Old, am I?" he grumbled. "That'll teach you to mess with old men, you knife-happy peckerwood," he said. He gave the body a sharp kick in the ribs for good measure.

"That's for Marcus Trevor," he said. It felt so good that he kicked the body again. "And for all those poor workin' gals, all those poor doves. I'd slice you up and feed you to the hogs, 'cept you'd taint the bacon."

Woolsey, who had so far remained silent, nodded happily and frantically scribbled on his pad, mouthing, "Taint the bacon. Oh, excellent, excellent!"

Garner whistled softly, and while Faro wandered over, he took a long drink of water from his canteen be-fore he thought of something.

"Hobie, frisk him. You're looking for a little silver locket. It was Annie Cartwell's." He hadn't forgotten, not for a slap second.

Hobie rolled the body over and found it in the third pocket he searched. He held it aloft, then tucked it care-fully into his coin purse along with Trevor's badge.

Satisfied, Garner stepped up into the saddle again, al-though quite a bit slower than usual. "Let's see if he hasn't murdered ol' Stealth, Hobie. I don't want the bas-tard's carcass bleedin' out over Faro's saddle."

22

It was a clear afternoon in September, just after a rain, and Garner was sitting on the porch doing the accounts. This was usually something he dreaded, mostly because he had to wear his glasses to see well enough to do it. But today the rain had perked him up enough that he was almost glad. Besides, the trees out across the valley were just beginning to turn. It was a good day to sit out on the porch and get something accomplished.

And then U.S. Marshal Holling Eberhart came splashing into the yard.

"Howdy, King," Eberhart said with a familiar grin and a wave. He was gray-haired and stocky, and probably ten years Garner's senior. It was Eberhart to whom Garner had reported the deaths of both Trevor and Martindale. He'd handed Belasco's corpse over to him, too. It was pretty smelly by that time.

Garner hurriedly snatched off his glasses and got to his feet. "Afternoon, Holling. What brings you out this way?"

Eberhart swung down off his horse and tethered it to the porch rail. "Just thought you might like to be brought up to date, King. About that Belasco mess, I mean."

"You could have written," Garner said.

"Needed to get off my ass and out of the office, anyhow," Eberhart said.

The screen door squeaked open, and Hobie, hands caught up in a dish towel, stuck his head out. "We got company, Boss?" he asked, before he brightened a bit, said, "How do, Marshal," and stuck out his hand.

Eberhart walked over to the table, and Hobie leaned back against the door frame, the dish towel slung over his shoulder. He was canning applesauce today, and the whole place smelled of cinnamon and sugar and pippins.

Eberhart pulled up a straight-backed chair and slung himself into it. "You got anything to drink, King? I'm pretty dusty."

"If you don't mind that it's soft," Garner replied, and Hobie, looking disappointed, sighed and went inside to fetch the sweet cider, screen door banging behind him.

"How's that grown daughter of yours, Holling?" Garner asked.

By the time Hobie returned and they had all downed a glass and gotten the small talk over with, Eberhart was ready to get down to it.

"Well, Marcus's wife took it awful hard," he said, lighting his pipe. "She cleared out and went back home to Kansas City. I bought that gray horse off her. He's a good one."

Garner just nodded. There wasn't much to say.

"Sent some boys out to pick up Trevor and what was left of Martindale," Eberhart went on, "and to go check on where Belasco got that pinto. Turned out it was a ranch. A mom and pop and a grown daughter, lost her husband last year to a diamondback." He puffed a moment, then shook his head. "They was mighty lucky. The two women were there alone the night that Belasco snuck in and took that pinto outta the corral. They'd best thank their lucky stars he was in a hurry and didn't take time to stop by the house."

"Amen," said Hobie, who had lingered.

"Now, King, I got a little business to talk over with you fellers," Eberhart said, and leaned forward just slightly.

Garner knew what he was going to say. He leaned away from Eberhart and tilted his head, scowling. "No."

"Now, how do you know what it is I'm gonna talk about?"

Garner set his glass down. "You asked me plenty of times before, and my answer's still the same. I know you boys have got some trouble, but—"

"Trouble?" said Eberhart, eyebrows hiked. "You don't know what trouble is. We lost Trevor. Between you and me it weren't much of a loss, but he was surely better than nothing. And I've lost two other men in the last month. Wasn't their fault. They were green as grass and I shouldn't have sent 'em out. I'll shoulder that blame. But dammit, King, about all I've got is green men, seems like. Now, wouldn't—"

"No."

Hobie took a step toward them. "Boss, is he askin' what I think he's askin'?"

"Stay outta this, Hobie," Garner growled. He wished he had a bottle of whiskey in the place, if only so that he could crack Eberhart over the head with it and knock some sense into him. The man knew better than to try and talk him into pinning on a badge again.

Eberhart held up both hands, palms out. "All right, all right," he said. "You don't need to go gettin' into a tizzy about it, King." He dropped his hands and sat back, frowning. "You boys hear about that Woolsey fella?"

"Hear what?" Hobie asked.

Eberhart turned toward him. "He got his story, Hobie, and bigger than he expected. The sonofabitch is writin' an exposé on the U.S. Marshals Service."

Garner burst out laughing.

"It's not funny, dammit!" Eberhart shouted. "That little no-ear peckerwood's writin' a series on us, about how we're all a bunch of showboatin' glory seekers and shouldn't be leechin' off the federal payroll."

Garner put a hand to his side. He hadn't heard anything so funny in a long time. Barely controlling his laughter, he said, "Serves you right, Holling. And why are you pickin' on a poor little boy with no head-handles?"

Eberhart scowled. "Bet you won't think it's so funny when you find out what he wrote about you."

Garner stopped laughing.

Eagerly, Hobie scraped out a chair quick and plopped down. "He wrote about us?"

"Oh, you're mentioned, Hobie," Eberhart said. "Just not by name."

Hobie's face fell.

"I think you're the one he refers to as 'the yellow-haired boy' or 'the fair youth.' Kind of a sidekick. But King here, mercy sakes alive!"

The expression on Eberhart's face was clear. The bastard was enjoying every minute of this.

Eberhart relit his pipe. "Now, King, here, is mentioned by name. Seems he led your party through the wilderness single-handed and with a blindfold on. Seems that while poor Marcus Trevor was bragging it up and getting lost and frolicking with saloon girls, and while whole towns was throwin' parties for him, ol' King here was on the job. 'A steadfast hero of the old school,' he wrote about King, and that's a quote."

"Don't be in such a hurry to leave, Holling," Garner said, and abruptly stood up.

"Did I say I was?" Eberhart asked innocently, and slung an arm over the back of his chair. "Good cider, Hobie, even if it ain't hard."

Garner sat back down again. "If you figure this is gonna help talk me into your offer, you're wrong."

"Ain't offered a thing, yet," Eberhart said, and poured himself another glass of cider. "Yessir, Hobie, awful good cider. Got a real tang to it. You use snow apples?"

"I use three kinds, Marshal," Hobie allowed. "I use those little pippins that grow—"

"Goddamn it, Holling!" Garner thundered so fast and loud that Hobie jumped a good foot. "You rode up here for a reason, and it wasn't to tell me about Marcus's widow or some damned article in the Tucson paper. So spit it out and I'll say no again, and then you can ride on back home."

Eberhart shook his head. To Hobie, he said, "Ain't too hospitable, is he?"

"He's been goin' over the accounts," Hobie confided. "That always makes him cranky."

"I'm not cranky!" Garner shouted.

"Quiet, King," Eberhart said genially. "It's Hobie I come to ask, anyhow, and I just asked you—or tried to, damn it—to be hospitable. You're too long in the tooth to be ridin' all over hell and gone anyhow, and we already got enough desk men. Hobie," he said, turning toward the boy, "how'd you like to be a special deputy marshal? Now, we wouldn't want you to—"

"Too long in the tooth?" Garner shouted. "You're a fine one to be callin' me that, you stinkin' old codger! Why, you rode with me down—"

"—go full-time, no, sir," Eberhart continued to Hobie, ignoring Garner entirely. "You could still work for King. This would be just for special times. You know, like when we get our tits caught in the wringer, as King here might put it."

"I can outtrack, outgun, and outthink you any day of the week, Holling Eberhart," King spat.

Eberhart turned toward him and gave a thoughtful scratch to the back of his neck. "Well, so you can, King, so you can. And I thank you for reminding me of it. Seems to me you're goin' to seed up here with nothin' to do but stare at them horses. No, I don't see anything holding me back from deputizin' you, too. Special-like, like Hobie, here."

Eberhart pulled a couple of badges, shiny and brandnew, from his pocket and put them on the table. "Might's well use you until you get so you can't ride no more. Squeeze the last drops of juice outta the lemon, so to speak."

"Listen here, Marshal," Hobie began, wide-eyed, "I never said as how—".

"You sonofabitch!" Garner bulled in. "I'm not going to put on any goddamn badge."

"If he's not goin' to, I ain't either," piped up Hobie.

"Been a long time since I swore anybody in without

my book," Eberhart mumbled, slapping at his pockets. "Dammit, I musta left it sittin' on my desk. . . ."

"And you're not goin' to start now," snapped an exasperated Garner.

Eberhart looked up. "Well, you boys promise to do your duty and obey the law of the land?"

"Well, of course we do that," yelped Hobie, who actually looked hurt. "We're law-abidin'. But that don't mean we want to—"

"Good." Eberhart picked up a badge and pinned it on Hobie's shirt. "And you, King?"

"Go to hell, Holling."

Eberhart nodded curtly. "Good enough for me. You can pin that on your own self, there, King." He scraped back his chair. "Well, I thank you kindly for the cider, boys. I'll be in touch."

"Hold on just a goddamn second, Holling," Garner said, standing. He scooped the badge up off the table, then ripped Hobie's off his shirt.

"Hey!" cried Hobie, more because his pocket was torn than anything else.

Garner jumped down the porch steps. "You take these back, Holling," he demanded.

But Eberhart, a big fat grin on his weathered face, was already up on his horse and backing it down the muddy yard. "Like I said, boys," he shouted around his pipe, "I'll be in touch."

He gave a wave, wheeled his horse around, and cantered on down the path and into the woods.

"Holling!" Garner shouted. And then he threw the badges down into the puddled yard. "I'll be a ring-tailed sonofabitch," he muttered.

Hobie came down the porch steps to stand beside him.

"And what do *you* want?" Garner roared.

Hobie blinked. "Nothin', Boss. 'Cept I don't reckon you should leave these lying around in the dirt and mud and such." He bent over and picked up the badges, gave them a wipe on his britches, then polished them on his shirt. "You know, you tore my pocket when you yanked this off."

"So fix it," Garner said. He was still staring after Eberhart.

Hobie eyed the badges thoughtfully. Garner could practically hear the wheels clicking. "Might be a while before I get time what with all these preserves I'm puttin' up," Hobie said. "Might be a real long while. So, until I do, I might just have to pin it together." He fastened the badge back on his chest, over the tear. "Yessir, that works real fine," he said, giving it a final rub with his sleeve. "You got any tears that need mendin', Boss?"

Garner glared at him. "Give that to me," he snapped, and tore the other badge from Hobie's hand.

"Better go and check my apples," Hobie said a little too happily, and started for the porch.

"Hobie?" Garner said.   .

Hobie stopped. "Yes, I think you're goin' to seed up here."

"What makes you think I was goin' to ask you that?"

"Weren't you?"

Garner snarled, "Aw, go check your goddamn apples."

Hobie grinned quite suddenly. "Yeah, Boss." He went inside, the screen door banging behind him.

Garner stood there a few moments, staring at the badge in his hand. Hobie had missed a spot, and he cleaned the last of the mud away on his sleeve. The badge was solid silver, and shone bright in the afternoon light. Hobie was right. It'd be a shame just to let it lie around out here in the yard.

But there was no way on God's green earth that Garner was going to let that old con artist Eberhart—or that whelp, Hobie—bamboozle him into putting on a badge again. So what if he was going to seed up here? It was his place, wasn't it? Where better to put down roots?

But then, the foals were weaned and halter-broke, and he couldn't do much with the yearlings until next summer. He'd already built all the fences and buildings he needed. If it wasn't for the feeding and mucking out stalls and checking the stock, he wouldn't even need Jim and Fred. Didn't hardly need the both of them now, and hell, they spent as much time in town as they did here.

He looked at the badge again, then closed his fingers over it.

"Aw, hell," he grumbled.

He slipped it into his pocket, then walked up the porch steps. Maybe he could do something for Holling. Just once. It would hold down the boredom. And it might be kind of nice, hitting the trail with Hobie. He was a good kid. Needed some seasoning, but he had promise. And he was reasonable company.

Garner sat down in his rocker once more and slipped on his reading glasses. "Too old, my ass," he muttered to himself. "And somebody remind me to swat that Woolsey if I ever run across him again." And then he turned and shouted, "Hobie! How long till dinner?"

"'Bout an hour, Boss," the kid called back. "And don't worry, I'll swat him first. Didn't even mention my name!"

Garner's lips curled into a barely perceptible grin. He pulled the stack of papers toward him, and got on with the accounts.